Acclaim for

THE SKYWORLD SERIES

"Treasure hunts and zombies sail smoothly in the skies of this post-apocalyptic world, raising natural questions about why such horrors and miseries exist . . . An enjoyable, well-crafted tale."

— LOREHAVEN MAGAZINE

"Morgan Busse's Skyworld series is an exciting steampunk duology you won't want to miss! A deadly mist, a daring heroine, and plenty of secrets collide for an action-packed adventure in the skies."

— S.D. GRIMM, author of the Children of the Blood Moon series

and *A Dragon by Any Other Name*

"A heart-pumping ride into the steampunk world of airships, searches for treasure, gunfights with the undead . . . with a gold masked automaton lurking in the shadows."

— JACQUELINE TOWNS, reviewer for H. Halverstadt Books

BLOOD SECRETS

Books by Morgan L. Busse

Follower of the Word series
Daughter of Light
Son of Truth
Heir of Hope

The Soul Chronicles
Tainted
Awakened

The Ravenwood Saga
Mark of the Raven
Flight of the Raven
Cry of the Raven

Skyworld series
Secrets in the Mist
Blood Secrets

SKYWORLD | BOOK TWO

BLOOD SECRETS

MORGAN L. BUSSE

ENCLAVE

Escape

To Caleb, my quiet adventurer.

May you discover all who God is.

1

THEO DRIFTED ALONG THE CURRENTS OF THE WIND with Cass tied to the front of him. She would move and moan, but she never woke up. Perhaps that was a good thing. He didn't want to be the one to tell her the *Daedalus* had burned and that they were all alone, drifting along the western mountain range with nothing but Theo's memories of the puzzle box and the papers he had found. The price for that knowledge seemed too high.

They had been gliding for hours when the sun began to set, spreading rays of orange and yellow across the Mist below. How much farther to Duskward? Every time the glider started to dip, he'd been fortunate to find an updraft, but he couldn't glide forever. He was cold, and his extremities were growing numb with chill, not to mention he hadn't eaten or drunk anything since yesterday. Adrenaline alone kept him going.

He glanced to his left. Should he try and land on the ragged mountains nearby and stay for the night? He squinted in the dying light. No, the cliffs were too steep, and one false landing would kill them—if he could even find a place to land. The western mountains were barren of humanity for a good reason: there was nowhere to live. And in his case, nowhere to land.

His only choice was to keep on gliding until they reached Duskward or the glider finally gave out.

Exhaustion crept across his body as his fingers stayed taut around the guiding poles. Every minute felt like an hour. His back hurt, his head hurt. Everything hurt. He forced his mind to focus elsewhere.

What were his sister Adora and Aunt Maude up to right now? He'd told them he'd be away for a while on business. Was his sister attending parties? Or spending her time with her charity work? Was Aunt Maude still grieving over Grandfather's death?

What about the *Daedalus*? The crew had to have escaped. Surely an airship like that had a plan of action in the event of a fire, right? But then, where had they gone?

One of Cass's curls drifted up and tickled the bottom edge of his cheek. What was he going to do with her? He'd lost the vial of blood that held the immunity to the Mist, but the woman tied to him carried that immunity inside of her. She could quite possibly be the salvation for humanity.

And the test subject for the House of Lords.

No. That was the one thing he wouldn't let happen.

He didn't trust them.

The sun sank below the horizon as stars appeared across the darkening sky. The natural beauty could not stop the sinking feeling in his chest. He dropped his head and closed his eyes. The heaviness expanded until it was hard to breathe. Was this it, then? Would he and Cass slowly coast back into the Mist, never to be heard from again?

Please, Elaeros, don't let it end this way. Don't—he thought of the House of Lords, and Luron, and all that had transpired so far—*don't let them win. Help me make it to Duskward.*

Theo let go of one of the guiding poles and brought his hand around and touched Cass's forehead. A burning fever encompassed her body, whether brought on by her exposure to the spores or something else.

His thoughts drifted over the last month and a half he'd spent with her. He still didn't know her background, not fully, but what he did know was she was smart, curious, and a fighter. She'd lived on the streets of Belhold for years, became a diver, and now even the spores from the Plague Wars couldn't take her out.

He longed to know her more. To introduce her to Adora. He had a feeling his sister would love this spunky young woman. He wanted to show her the lab below the manse and the Winchester library. He could almost envision her green eyes brighten with curiosity and the flood of questions. Never once had there been the type of tedious conversation he usually experienced with his peers—both men and women—with Cass. She had a mind of her own. One that matched his.

Just as the last ray of light died from the sky, a cluster of small twinkling lights appeared along the mountainside. Relief spread through Theo as he steered the glider toward the lights. They had made it.

The weeks and months ahead would be filled with peril: from Luron and the House of Lords, danger from illness, the cost of finding a cure, and so much more. But for now, he'd welcome this small victory. Tomorrow would take care of itself.

Theo glided along the wind, careful to slow down his speed while staying above the village. As he drew closer, he could see the cluster of buildings and walkways built along the side of the mountain. Lamps hung from poles that lined the wooden planks. It wouldn't be easy to land on the narrow ledges, but given everything he'd experienced so far, he wasn't about to let something like that stop him. He gripped the poles tighter and steered for the widest walkway that went through the village, using the illumination from the lamps to light his way. Down, down . . .

He brought the tip of the glider up just enough to stall, then landed on his feet. Cass slumped forward like a rag doll. A handful of people started to emerge from the wooden homes.

Ignoring the gathering crowd, Theo put the guiding poles away, then pulled on the cord at his side. The glider began to collapse as it gathered inside his pack until, with a soft click, it was neatly folded and compact. He pulled his goggles up, unstrapped his mask, then worked on Cass's connecting cord.

Murmurs filled the shadowed areas. A lanky man with grey-streaked hair pulled back at the nape of his neck approached him. "What's going on here?" he asked. "And who in the Mist are you?"

Theo undid the clip and let the cord fall. How did he explain everything that had transpired over the last twenty-four hours? He looked up. "My name is Byron. My companion and I have been investigating a town in the Mist for the last couple of days. When we ascended skyward, we discovered our airship was on fire. We had no choice but to glide to the nearest town. Yours was the closest. We've been in the air since almost noon today."

The man's eyes widened. "Noon? You've been gliding for over six hours?"

"Yes." Theo kept one hand around Cass while he worked the ropes that tied them together.

"Six hours," someone repeated. "That's crazy."

"More like insane."

"Is that even possible?"

The lanky man came closer. "What's wrong with your companion?"

"A fever." Theo looked up. "Do you have a doctor here?"

"Nope. Just us folks on the brink of civilization. But we do have a midwife. She knows enough."

"Can you take us to her?"

"Certainly. Tom, Andrew, help that man out."

Two more men stepped out from the shadows. Theo worked the last knot with chilled fingers, fumbling once. His teeth began to chatter. If he didn't warm up soon, he might catch a fever as well. And that would not be good.

As soon as the knot came undone, Cass slumped forward, and her pack hit the walkway. The two men caught her by the shoulders. "T-thank you," Theo said as a convulsion of shivers took over. Now that he'd reached solid ground, his body was giving out on him.

"Take 'em to my house. I'll get Hettie," the lanky man said and disappeared into the darkness.

"Who is that man?" Theo asked the other two.

"Sam Burton. You could say he's the mayor of our small village. Oversees the running of Duskward," the shorter one said. "I'm Andrew and that there is Tom. His son."

"I'll take the young woman to my father's house." Before Theo could respond, Tom scooped up Cass. "Follow me." He headed up the walkway. Theo snatched Cass's pack and followed along with Andrew.

Tall thin houses lined either side of the walkway, with narrow glass windows where light trickled out. Boards creaked under their boots. Beyond the row of houses, the sheer cliff of the western mountains rose.

Near the middle of the village, signs hung from broader buildings: mercantile, clothier, and even a barbershop. Tom stopped in front of a two-story home just past the mercantile and knocked on the door.

Seconds later, a hefty older woman opened the door. "Tom? Is that you?" She peered into the darkness. "Oh my, who're you carrying?"

"Father sent us. Travelers. This one's sick. Father told us to bring her here while he went to get Hettie."

She stepped back. "Yes, yes, bring her in."

They walked in, and the woman gave Theo a cursory glance before gathering up her skirts and leading the way up a set of stairs just beyond the foyer.

The house was simple and clean, with ivory walls and grass-green trim, floral rugs, and a round clock ticking the time on the far wall. The wooden stairs creaked as they ascended to the next floor. "In here." The lady opened the nearest door and ushered them through. The interior was dark, but Theo could make out a single bed with a white coverlet in the corner. A dresser stood against the opposite wall with a gas lamp on top.

Tom laid Cass on the bed while the woman lit the lamp. She was a well-rounded woman, with her grey hair pulled up and covered by a white cap. The lines along her face told of a well-lived life. "So what exactly is going on?" she asked.

Theo could feel his body thawing out in the warmth of the house. "As Tom said, we are travelers. Divers actually."

"Is your ship docked here?"

Theo's chest clenched. "No. On our way out of the Mist, we discovered it was on fire, and so we glided to the nearest town."

Her eyes widened. "You glided here?" She glanced at Cass. "And this young woman?"

"She has a fever and has been unconscious. I attached her to me to get here."

"That is quite a story." She turned. "While Sam's getting Hettie, I'll change her out of those cold garments and get her into bed. I have an old nightgown that will do. When I've taken care of her, I'll see what I can do about you," she said, eyeing Theo. "Now out, all three of you."

The young men stepped into the hallway, and the door shut behind them. Theo swayed on his feet and dropped Cass's glider to the floor.

"Whoa." Tom grabbed him by the arm.

"Sorry." Theo brushed the side of his head. "I haven't eaten anything for two days now."

"Then let's take you to the kitchen and get you something."

Theo could only give a weak nod.

2

"SO BYRON, EH?"

Theo barely registered Tom's remark as he took a long draught of water from a wooden cup, then bit into a slice of bread with a thick layer of mountain-berry jam on top. He felt a rush of gratification. He'd never gone without food for this long before. It sobered him to think that Cass might have once been very familiar with this feeling.

"Yes." He looked up and swallowed. "Byron." With Luron and perhaps the House of Lords searching for him, he was certainly not going to reveal his real name.

The kitchen was cozy, with a long wooden table taking up most of the space. Green-painted cupboards hung along two of the walls, wooden counters underneath. An old cast-iron stove had a kettle on top. A large loaf of bread sat on a cutting board, half of it now piled on a plate before Theo along with a crock of jam. Long narrow windows revealed the darkness of the coming night.

"Where are you from, Byron?"

Theo took another bite before answering. "Belhold."

"And you're a diver?"

"Temporary one. My companion is the professional."

Tom leaned in with a curious look on his face. "So what happened?"

"Like I said, we were coming up from a dive and found our ship on fire. Cass, the other diver, had taken sick during the dive, and so I was ascending with her. When I discovered our vessel engulfed in flames, I knew my only option was to locate a place to land above the Mist. As you know, there are very few places along the western mountains."

Tom nodded thoughtfully. "Still, to have come all the way to Duskward." He frowned. "Where exactly were you diving?"

"A city south of here."

"Did you run into any Turned?"

Theo placed his slice of bread down. "Yes."

The look on his face must have alerted the other to the fact that he didn't want to talk about it.

Tom stood up. "Lots of Turned around here," he said. "Old ones. No one knows why. We had a ship come by a couple months ago and dive down into the village below us. Heard there was a mishap and they lost their captain and one of the crew."

Theo was instantly alert. "What was the name of the ship?"

"The Daddling? Daddler? Something like that. They were in my father's mercantile, stocking up on supplies before the dive. Risky business, diving."

The door down the hall opened, and the sound of boots and voices of a man and woman echoed through the house.

"Well, it appears Father's back with Hettie. I should head home. Best of luck to you, Byron."

"And to you, Tom."

Tom waved without turning around as he left the kitchen.

Theo finished the last slice of bread and the rest of his water before heading out into the hallway. He spotted Sam and his wife talking near the door while an older and much shorter woman made her way up the staircase.

Sam turned toward him. "We hardly ever get travelers here. And those who visit come with their own ship or means of travel.

Since you have no ship, the missus and I have been talking and would like to extend to you a place to stay for the night."

Theo inclined his head. "Thank you for your kindness. I accept with much appreciation."

"I'll start preparing your room." Mrs. Burton said and went back up the stairs.

"I wanted to let you know the courier will be here tomorrow," Sam informed him. "He uses one of those new aeroships. Maybe there's a chance he could take you and your companion back to your city."

Aeroship? Theo had heard about them. They were a more recent invention. Instead of using bags of gas to keep the ship afloat, aeroships were built with sleek designs to cut a swath through the air and could travel three to four times the speed of a dirigible. Instead of taking a couple weeks, it would only take a day or two to reach Belhold. If they could catch a ride with this courier, it would throw Luron and the House of Lords off their scent, at least for a while. A real doctor could watch over Cass while Theo figured out what to do next, who to talk to, and what to do about her blood.

Of course, that brought a whole slew of questions regarding Cass, science, and ethics. Where did one begin and one end when humankind was on the line?

"I would greatly appreciate that," Theo told him. "And for your help and lodging, I will be more than happy to repay you when I arrive home."

Sam waved his hand. "No need. It's not often we receive travelers here, especially ones with such an interesting story."

A minute later, Mrs. Burton came back down the stairs. "I have your room prepared, Mister . . ."

"Byron."

"Byron. I've heard that name before." She thought for a moment, then shook her head. "Your room is ready."

Theo grabbed the glider packs and ascended to the second floor after her. He stopped by the closed door that led to the room where they had laid Cass. "Any news?"

"Not yet. But when there is, I'll be sure to tell you." Mrs. Burton led him to the room next door. "There are fresh linens on the bed, and I'll bring up a pitcher of water for cleaning."

The room looked similar to the one Cass occupied, with a pale coverlet, a dresser, and a simple rug on the wooden floor. The lamp beside the small bed had been lit.

Theo dropped the packs on the floor, then collapsed on the bed. He closed his eyes. Every muscle in his body ached. He could feel the dents along his cheeks and jaw from the gas mask. But he and Cass had made it. They were alive.

They weren't out of the woods yet, so to speak. Cass was still under the ravages of a fever, Luron was still out there, and there was a mountain of research to do when he arrived back at Belhold. But if he was successful, there might actually be a cure for the Mist.

A cure that currently resided in the young woman next door.

3

THE FIRST THING CASS WAS AWARE OF WAS HER BODY vibrating and a loud buzzing in her ears. And heat. As if she were trapped inside the fire barrier during a Purge. Maybe she was. The last thing she remembered was a dozen Turned surrounding her while she fired off every incendiary bullet she had before blacking out.

She tried to open her eyes, but she was so weak even that was hard. After a moment, she was able to pry them open and look around. She was inside some kind of metal container, like an oversized coffin.

At the thought, she tried to sit up, and her vision went dark for a moment. A splitting headache tore across her head. "Where am I?" she croaked.

An arm steadied her. "You're safe, Cass. Don't worry."

"Theo?"

"Yes."

"Where are we?"

"Inside an aeroship."

"An aeroship?" Her eyes closed. Already the heated darkness was threatening to take over again.

"We're heading back to Belhold."

She tried to clear her mind. How in the Mist were they heading back to Belhold when the last thing she could recall was escaping the village of Voxhollow? How had they gotten away? Where had Theo found this aeroship, and why weren't they on the *Daedalus*?

The *Daedalus*!

She tried to squirm and Theo gently laid her back. "The *Daedalus*. Why aren't we on the *Daedalus*?"

Theo placed a hand on her arm. "That is a long story, and I'll tell you once we reach Belhold. But for now, you need to rest. You're very sick."

That would explain the heat and achiness.

The hand came to rest on her forehead. His touch felt cool against her hot skin. The vibrations from the aeroship and the constant buzz pulled her back into a slumbering void.

Hours passed as she drifted in and out of sleep. Theo was a constant presence during those brief periods of consciousness. After a while, the buzzing and vibrations stopped. She felt someone lift her up and carry her out into the cold air. The little she could see convinced her it was night. Then she drifted back to sleep.

"I GAVE HER AMITAINE AND A SEDATIVE TO HELP HER sleep. If all proves well, her fever should break sometime over the next twenty-four hours. But she'll be very weak and will need to take it easy for a couple of days if not longer."

"Thank you, Dr. Turner," Cass heard Theo say.

"Of course. Also, make sure she receives plenty of liquids. I'll come back next week to see how she's doing. However, if anything changes, don't hesitate to send for me."

"I will."

There was the sound of muffled boots and a door closing. Cass let out a weak breath and turned her head. Something soft touched her cheek. Drawn to the comfort, she turned on her side and snuggled into the billowy softness. Somewhere in the back of her mind, she identified it as a pillow, but not one she had ever experienced before. Seconds later, an equally soft coverlet was pulled up to her chin, and she sighed. She still felt like she was on fire, but the cool pillow and coverlet were traces of heaven in the heat. Maybe she was suspended between the two planes of death, lingering, unable to proceed up or down.

That was a disturbing thought. If that were true, then where was Elaeros? Did the actions of her life warrant heaven . . . or hell?

"HERE YOU GO."

Cass felt her head tip upward, and something that tasted like chicken broth dribbled into her mouth. "That's it. Drink up."

That voice did not belong to Theo. It was a woman's, and it sounded like sunshine and laughter. Cass opened her eyes and found a young woman bending over her with a bowl in her hand. Her golden hair was pulled back, and the light streaming in from a window behind her made it appear as if a halo surrounded her beautiful face.

"One more sip, alright?"

Cass nodded weakly and took the broth when the bowl touched her lips. The bowl drew away, and Cass watched as the young woman placed it on the nightstand. "Who are you?" she asked.

"My name is Adora. I'm Theo's sister."

Cass blinked. "His sister?" She turned her head across the pillow. "Where am I? And how did I get here?"

"Theo brought you to our home. You were very sick, so I doubt you remember much of anything at all."

"Oh." Cass tried to recall more, but nothing came.

Adora smiled. "Rest now. I'll be back in a little while to check on you."

Cass attempted to smile back, but that required too much energy. "Thank you."

"Of course." Adora stood and smoothed the wrinkles from her dark-blue gown. "Is there anything else I can do for you?"

Cass closed her eyes. The heat was gone, but it had left behind a bone-aching fatigue. "No. Thank you."

She heard Adora move across the room. "Then I'll let you sleep."

Cass had no idea what time it was or how long she had been here, wherever Theo's home was. But there was one thing she was sure of: she was safe. If Adora was anything like her brother—and she appeared to be so—Cass would be taken care of. As much as she had always been independent, right now she needed the help of others.

4

THE NEXT DAY, CASS COULD MANAGE TO GET UP AND was even able to move about the room. If the light coming through the window was any indication, it was early afternoon. She stood by the glass panes. The sunshine felt wonderfully warm against her chilled body. She looked out the window and frowned. Was that . . . a cloud?

A slip of white cotton drifted about twenty feet away. Cass looked down and her eyes went wide. An expansive lawn spread from the edge of the house to a stone wall that surrounded the property. And beyond the wall, down far below, was the city of Belhold.

Cass took a quick step back from the window. A sky island. This house was built on one of the sky islands that hovered above Belhold. How many times had she looked up and watched the small islands float by, wondering how rich someone had to be to live on one?

Were the Byrons really that wealthy? A vague statement issued by the metal man came to mind. She tried to recall his words, but that whole time remained fuzzy, and it just made her head pound.

The door opened behind her. Cass turned as the young blond

woman from yesterday entered the room.

"Cass, you're awake!" the young woman exclaimed.

Cass frowned. What was her name again?

The young woman gave an understanding smile. "I'm Adora," she said as she walked over to Cass. She wasn't as tall as her brother, but she was still a good few inches taller than Cass. "I had a bath drawn for you, and I think I might have a skirt and blouse that will be sufficient for now."

Cass glanced down at her current attire. The dress she was wearing was a faded blue and much too big on her. She glanced around the room. Where was her corset? Her blouse? And trousers? "Where are my own things?" she asked.

"Your clothes? I'm currently having them washed."

Cass pinched the fabric and rubbed it between her fingers. What in the world happened to her? One person would know. "Where's Theo?"

"He's not available right now. He paced the hallway outside your room all night until your fever broke. And he would still be here if I hadn't sent him away to rest. I've never seen him so agitated." Adora glanced at her with a glint in her eye and a half smile on her face.

Cass wanted to see him as soon as possible to get answers for the myriad of questions in her head. But it sounded like he needed rest as much as she did. Her questions would have to wait.

"Bathe first," Adora said kindly. "You'll feel much better afterward."

Cass ran a hand across her hair. The strands were as curly as ever, and tangled. And her skin felt grimy. It would be nice to clean up. She realized the last time she had washed up was on the *Daedalus*. Speaking of, where was the *Daedalus*? Just another question she would have for Theo once she saw him.

Cass followed Adora out into the hall. The last time she had used an actual bath, it was a tiny barrel that her parents would haul into their flat. After that, washing was a luxury on the streets saved for rainy days. And a pitcher and bowl sufficed on the *Daedalus*.

The bottom half of the hallway was paneled in a rich warm wood. Ivory wallpaper covered the upper half. Cass let her fingertips brush the wallpaper. Textured. And beautiful.

They passed four doors until they reached the end of the hall, where a large window overlooked the lawn and city below.

Adora opened the door for her. "Feel free to use anything you like. I placed the soap next to the bath."

Cass peered inside. The room was small and everything was tiled in white. A sink stood beneath a square window. To the right was a commode and to the left a porcelain tub, steam rising from within.

After the door shut behind her, Cass marveled at the room on closer inspection. Everything needed for cleanliness in one place. So this was what it was like to be an echelon.

She stepped toward the bath and placed a finger in the water. Perfect temperature. She went over to the sink. Two knobs were stationed at the top, one with the letter *C*, the other with the letter *H*. She twisted the *H* knob. Water began to pour out of the spout below. She touched the water.

"Ouch!" She jerked back her hand. The water was hot!

She turned the knob and the water stopped. Amazing.

The bath beckoned her. She pulled off the oversized dress and sank into the warm water. What a luxury. So much water, and so soothing. She spent minutes soaking in the warmth, then reached for the bar of soap. A rose scent drifted from it. She held it to her nose and breathed in the smell. Even the soap was beyond anything she knew. She scrubbed every inch of her body and hair until the water turned grey and cloudy and the small room smelled like roses.

So this was how Theo lived. With entire rooms dedicated to

bathing. She shook her head in wonder. Despite the cleansing and comfort, exhaustion crept back. Just walking down the hallway and bathing seemed to have taken everything out of her. She climbed out and reached for the large white cloth to dry off.

Seconds later, there was a knock at the door. Cass gripped the cloth to her body. "Yes?"

"I have clean clothes for you," a feminine voice said.

Cass looked around, then back at the door. "Go ahead and leave them."

"Yes, miss." There was a shuffle, then the hall was quiet again.

Carefully Cass opened the door and found the mentioned folded clothing. She grabbed them and quickly shut the door. The starch-white undergarments, stockings, long dark skirt, and white blouse were a bit big on her, but she was able to cinch up the skirt. She wasn't sure what to do with the faded blue dress, so she folded it and placed it over a wooden chair. She emerged from the bathing room to find Adora standing in the hallway.

"Oh good, they fit," Adora said with a bright smile. Her eyes were identical to Theo's: dark and rich. And she had the same nose and high cheekbones. But unlike Theo's dark hair, hers was blond, like the sun, and currently pulled back in a fashionable chignon. "Come. Hannah is waiting in the guest room to do your hair."

"My hair?" Cass felt one of her curls. Her hair was partly dry already since it was fairly short. Long hair attracted unwanted attention and was more work than she cared for, so she always kept her hair at shoulder's length.

"Yes." Adora glanced back. "It's a beautiful color."

Cass blinked. No one had ever said that to her before.

Back in the guest room, an older woman was waiting near

a chair in the middle of the room with a brush in hand. Her clothes were dark and simple, and her hair pulled back into a severe bun.

"Cass, this is our housekeeper, Hannah."

The older woman dipped her chin. "Miss."

Cass hoped the housekeeper wasn't going to style her hair in the same rigid manner. Then again, her hair was much too wild for that.

After she sat down, Hannah started working her hair. Adora came to stand nearby. "I'm afraid I don't know much about you. My brother has not been very forthcoming in answers."

"What do you want to know?"

Adora hesitated. "To be honest, I don't know where my brother has been for the last few weeks. He went away on business, then came home a couple nights ago with you. That in itself is strange. Theo usually keeps to himself, or hides in his labs. All I know is your name and that you needed our help."

Had Theo not told his family what he was doing? Perhaps there was a reason for his silence. If so, she wouldn't say anything until she knew why. "I'm a diver for the *Daedalus*. Your brother hired our ship for a diving mission."

"A diver?" Adora opened, then closed her mouth. "I wonder what Theo was looking for . . ."

Cass was silent as Hannah worked with her hair.

Adora eyed her curiously. "How did you become a diver? Most women of my acquaintance do not work."

Cass cast a glance around the room. She wasn't surprised. Given the beautiful furnishings, the wallpaper, the wood paneling, and the fact that this manse was located on a sky island, no woman of Adora's station would work.

Before she could answer, a muffled ring sounded from the hallway. Adora glanced at the door and sighed. "I'm sorry, Cass. I'm expecting company, and it would seem they have arrived early. However"—she smiled—"I do want to hear your story. It sounds exciting." She lifted her skirt and left the room as Hannah finished.

"There," the housekeeper said. "That should suffice."

There was a small mirror above the dresser. Cass stood and approached it. She reached up and tentatively touched the loose rolls on either side of her face and the back of her neck where her curls were captured. Somehow Hannah had tamed her wild, unruly hair into a sophisticated look, making her appear almost like a lady.

"Thank you," she said gratefully.

Hannah inclined her head, a hint of a smile on her face. "My pleasure. While you were bathing, Master Theo asked for you. He's waiting in the study on the first floor. I'll show you the way."

Cass's heart did a flip flop inside her chest. She hadn't spoken to Theo since Voxhollow, not really. Those hazy moments during her fever-induced wakefulness didn't count. All she knew was that he had saved her and brought her back to Belhold.

Cass followed the housekeeper through the hallway and down the grand staircase. As they made their way through the house, Cass noticed that instead of paintings, framed documents hung along the wall. She looked at the closest one, and her eyes widened.

Crispin Jules Winchester.

Winchester?

The next one had the name *David Crispin Winchester.* There was even a woman's name: *Phoebe Eliza Winchester.*

"Excuse me, Hannah. Who are all these people?"

The housekeeper glanced up. "They are notable members of the Winchester family."

Cass's steps faltered. "Winchesters? But I thought this was the Byron family."

"Oh, no, Miss. This is the Winchester manse."

Cass felt suddenly chilled. This wasn't the Byron manse. This was the Winchester house. Winchester, one of the powerful Five Families, highest of echelons, and head of the Alchemy Society.

"So Theo's last name isn't Byron?" She hoped she was wrong.

"No." Hannah glanced at her with a puzzled look. "It's Winchester. Master Theodore Winchester. He is the head of the Winchester family."

Cass's heart stopped. Theo had lied to her.

5

THEO HEARD THE DOOR OPEN BEHIND HIM. FOR ONE brief moment, he wondered if Adora was bringing her guests in to greet him. Not today, he thought as he gripped the book tighter in his hand. Then he heard a familiar voice.

"Theo?"

Theo rose quickly to his feet.

Cass stood in the doorway, dressed in a white blouse and long dark skirt. Her usual wild and curly hair had been captured, twisted, and pinned back, leaving wisps of rose-gold curls along her neck. The sunlight streaming in through the windows set between the bookcases brought out her bright green eyes.

Something flashed across those eyes as she crossed her arms. "Just who exactly are you, Theo?"

He hadn't even had a chance to ask how she was feeling. "What do you mean?"

"You said your name was Byron. But I saw the names in the hallway." She crossed the room and stared up into his face. "So who are you really?"

Theo swallowed. This was not how he wanted to disclose his family's name. But he should have known Cass would figure things out.

"Well?"

Theo took a breath and motioned to the chair across from where he had been sitting. "Please, take a seat."

"No. I want an answer now."

Theo hesitated, then went around her to shut the door to the study.

"I never lied to you." He picked up the book he had dropped on the chair. "My name *is* Theodore Byron. But Byron is not my last name. My surname is Winchester."

A heavy silence hung in the air. Theo placed the book carefully on a small table between the chairs.

"Why did you lie about your name?"

"For many reasons, Cass," he replied. "I wanted to keep my research and trip to Voxhollow a secret. And because I didn't want you to know who I really was."

"But why?" He could hear the hurt in Cass's voice. "Why the deception? Why not use your family's name? 'Winchester' would have provided you with many things."

Theo looked directly at her. "Yes, my name has the ability to open doors, but it also can close many others. Let me ask you, if you knew I was a Winchester, how would you have reacted?"

"I wouldn't have liked you," Cass admitted. "You were already an echelon when we met. The name Winchester would have only made me think even more badly of you."

Theo nodded. "Exactly. And everyone on the *Daedalus* would have viewed me likewise. I also didn't want the House of Lords knowing about my mission to Voxhollow. But somehow someone found out anyway."

"So, the House of Lords is against you?"

Theo laughed humorlessly. "They've always been against a cure."

"What do you mean?"

"Those in power like their power. If a cure were found and

people were released from the cities to live across the lands and valleys, they would be harder to control. To use. But if everyone is trapped on the mountaintops with the fear of the rising Mist and Purges, those in power can do what they want."

She was silent for a moment. "I still don't like the fact that you lied to me."

"I don't, either." He was amazed at how strongly he felt about that.

"I'm not sure what to think," Cass said slowly. "But I think I understand your reasoning." She shook her head. "A Winchester." Her tone held disbelief.

He smiled at her suddenly. "It's not all that bad?"

Cass gave a slight shrug, then returned his smile with a small one of her own. "Well, Cass isn't my full name, either."

He arced an eyebrow. "Really?"

"Cass is my nickname. I've never told anyone my real name."

Well, this was curious. Was this her way of lightening the mood? He would play along. "Then is it Cassandra?"

"No."

"Cassidy?"

"No."

"I give up. What is it?"

"Cassiopeia."

Theo's mouth twitched.

"I guess my parents had a flair for the extravagant," Cass said and looked at him. "Not everyone is named after an ancient queen."

"That's true," Theo said. "And your surname?"

Cass shook her head. "I don't have one."

"You don't?"

"No. Many of us on the streets don't. Or if we do, it's just one of our parents' names."

"So what were your parents' names?"

Her face grew somber, and she looked down as she pulled out the small silver locket she always wore around her neck. "Silas and Sara."

"That locket means a lot to you," Theo said softly.

"It was my mother's. She gave it to me the night they hid me from the Purges."

Theo had never heard the details of her family or early life. "How did you escape?"

Cass lowered her head and quietly shared with him the night the Purges came and took her parents. Silence fell across the study when she finished.

"My parents died looking for a cure for the Mist," he said moments later.

Her head rose, and he told her of the crashed zipper.

He watched the changing expression of her eyes. Compassion, concern, then a flicker of curiosity. "Theo, what happened to me back in Voxhollow?"

"How far back do you remember?"

"I remember running, and the metal man. And you handed me the puzzle box." Her brows creased. "I'm sorry, Theo. I think I lost the box."

"It's alright. I know what was inside. I was able to open it the night before and read through the contents. There was also a vial of blood."

"Blood?" Cass wrinkled her nose.

"Yes. Apparently there are a handful of people who are immune to the Mist."

"What does that mean?"

"They don't Turn. The metal man who was chasing us is one of them."

"People who don't Turn?" Cass said, eyes wide. "How is that possible?"

"I believe it has to do with a person's blood. The Mist spores spread across the body by blood. But if a person's blood blocks the spores, they can't spread. And the person wouldn't Turn."

Cass blinked. "And that metal man is one of those people with 'special blood'? Does he know he's immune?"

"Yes. The mask he was wearing was only to cover his face, not protect against the spores."

"Can his blood be used to help others?"

"I believe so." He wouldn't burden her with the fact that the House of Lords was unwilling to explore the idea.

"But he's gone now." Cass let out a long sigh. "So we're back to where we started."

"Not quite. There is another who carries this immunity. When I found you in the woods outside Voxhollow, your mask was no longer on your face."

It took a moment for his words to register. "My mask?"

"Yes. It was dangling from one ear."

"That's not possible," she whispered. "I've seen what happens to those who breathe in the Mist. I watched Captain Gresley turn with my own eyes. There must be some mistake."

"There is no mistake. The moment I picked you up, your mask fell to the ground."

Her face grew pale and her pupils swallowed up the green of her eyes. "Tell me everything."

6

CASS REMAINED VERY STILL WHILE THEO SHARED everything from that day, including the fate of the *Daedalus*.

"The *Daedalus*," she whispered. She wiped away the few tears that had fallen. "I don't understand. My parents, and those in the Purges, and Captain Gresley, and Oliver, they all Turned. How did I live when so many people died?"

"I suspect your blood is the answer. Just like the masked man."

"But why now? Why me?" An array of emotions swept over her face, and for one moment, he thought she would cry or scream or both. Her face went from red to white, her lips tightened, and her eyes held a fiery glint. Then her shoulders sagged as if whatever battle she had been waging inside had subsided.

Seconds later, Cass looked up. "All my life has been about moving forward, about surviving." She let out a deep, shaky breath. "So what do we do next?"

Theo marveled at her resilience. Not many would be able to look ahead after hearing such shocking news. "My expertise is on the Mist, not the human body," he began. "I could figure out why the spores don't affect you, but I wouldn't know what to do after that. However, I might have some connections at the university that may lead us someone who could discover how to use your immunity to help the rest of us."

"So if my blood holds a possible solution, then whoever that is will need some to experiment with."

"Yes."

"Will it hurt?"

"Well, I don't think we will be bloodletting," Theo said with a reassuring smile. "I've heard of a way to extract blood with a tiny needle and directly place it into a glass vial. I think that would be a better way."

Cass started to pale again. Theo was used to talking about such things with his grandfather and colleagues, but Cass wasn't. He went on quickly. "But first, we need to contact someone who has more knowledge in this area than I do."

"Who?"

"A professor of mine from Browning."

"Can you trust this person?"

Theo paused. His last conversation with Professor Hawkins almost a year ago hadn't gone as he had planned, but he didn't really have anyone else he could turn to, not at the moment. He needed to try again. "Yes, I believe so."

"When will you go?"

Theo sat back. Terms would be starting at Browning. The professor should already be back at the school. "Hopefully this week."

"And what should I do in the meantime?"

He wanted to say *rest*, but knew Cass wouldn't do that. Honestly, he wouldn't either, not when they were so close to unlocking a possible cure for the Mist. Cass needed to be kept occupied. She could be of some help in the laboratory. "How would you feel about assisting me?"

A spark came to her eyes and she nodded. "I would like that."

She seemed lost in thought after that. Her expression changed. Her eyes fixated on nothing he could see. She finally spoke. "Theo. About the *Daedalus*." He felt a rush of emotion as she looked at him, eyes shimmering again. "A fire wouldn't take out the crew. We had safeguards in place for such an event."

Theo didn't want to discourage her, but he couldn't see that there was any hope in that. Even if everyone had gliders, where would they have gone? And if the masks had been fitted with the new filters, they would only last at the most three days below.

"But I'm not sure where the crew would go," she continued. "Would it be possible to find out anything? Usually when we're looking for information, we post it in places along the docks of multiple cities. I—" her cheeks reddened. "I'm afraid I don't have the sterlings for those ads at the moment. So if I could borrow some money—"

"I'll do it."

"I'll pay you once I find a job," Cass said quickly.

"Since the *Daedalus* was destroyed while under my employment, I think it's only right that I cover the costs." Cass went to open her mouth to protest, but Theo raised his hand. "Cass, I care about the crew, too. I want to find out what happened to them. And if there is anything I can possibly do for them, I will."

Cass closed her mouth, but he could still see the conflict on her face.

Don't be stubborn, Cass. Let me do this one thing for you.

The clock ticked off each second as he waited. Finally, she spoke. "Alright. But please inform me of anything you discover."

"Of course." He stood up and held a hand out to her. She took it and stood there beside him. "I'll place those notices as soon as possible. And then we'll start working in my lab."

Her eyebrows shot up. "Lab?"

He grinned. "Yes. I have my own private lab here."

She shook her head. "You know, you're not at all what I thought an echelon was like."

He looked back at her, face serious now. "Cass, my father used to tell me our blessings weren't only for us, but to be shared with others. I'm glad I have the money and resources now to help however I can. Whoever I can."

Cass smiled. "I like that."

7

THE NEXT MORNING A SUMMER STORM CRASHED across Belhold. Theo watched the rain pound across the window inside the study before turning back to the pile of papers on his desk. As much as he wanted to visit the dead zone and check the rising Mist, it was too risky to try and take out a zipper in this downpour and wind. So instead, he threw himself into his next project: recalling the information from the puzzle box and all of the notes he had accumulated while on the *Daedalus*, which had subsequently burned in the inferno along with his microscope. Notes, drawings, knowledge, anything he could remember, he put to pen and parchment. When his brain had finally had enough, he checked on a handful of slides of deceased spores. There wasn't much to learn that he didn't already know, but this would give him a starting point again.

After spending yesterday in his lab and exhausting all her questions, Cass now sat in a chair opposite his desk in the study, her knees pulled up under her, and a book in her hands. She hadn't said a word since she'd started and seemed so enthralled; he wondered if she knew he was still in the room.

He smiled as he watched her read, then the smile slowly slipped away. Aunt Maude didn't know what to make of Cass and made it obvious she didn't like Cass's intrusion on their family. Twice during the evening meal last night, Theo had to delicately reprimand his aunt.

"She doesn't belong here." Aunt Maude had spoken to Theo alone in the hallway later that evening. "A working woman in our home? With no family?"

"She's a diver, Aunt Maude," Theo replied. "An honest job that has supported her since she has no family." Aunt Maude was caught in the web of haves and have-nots that plagued not only Belhold, but all of the lands in the sky. She couldn't see how she and Cass were actually in similar situations, only that his aunt had the Winchester name and fortune to sustain her, while Cass only had her wits.

Adora, on the other hand, loved Cass.

"It is refreshing to have another female mind with which to engage in intelligent conversation," Adora said as she poured tea later that afternoon. The storm continued to rage outside. Cass had chosen to lay down and rest.

"Oh, you've been talking to Cass?"

"Yes. I spoke to her last night in the library."

"What about all your friends?"

Adora shrugged. "You already know. Friends are wonderful for parties and shopping, but fashion, food, and eligible bachelors are the only things they talk about." She gave him a sidelong glance as she put the teapot down. "Cass reminds me of you."

"What do you mean?"

His sister laughed, a wonderful full-throat laugh that Theo always thought sounded like sunshine and everything good. "She's curious, she's seen far more of the world than I have, and her mind is quick. I'm sure you're the reason she's reading that Daniel Jacobs book. Am I correct?"

"Well, once she realized there was more to read than primers, I couldn't stop her."

She smiled. "I caught her glancing over the human anatomy book on the table nearby. None of my friends would ever read such a thing."

"Cass once told me she wants to discover everything there is to know."

"Just like my brother," Adora remarked fondly. "You two make a good team."

He rubbed the back of his neck. "Yes, I suppose so."

He hadn't told Adora everything. He didn't want to put his sister in danger. But he couldn't keep Cass here forever. And eventually Adora would need to know. Someday whoever had sent Luron after him would realize he was still alive and come after him again. "I'm going to head down to Browning this week."

She looked at him, teacup in midair. "You're going back to school?"

"Not yet. I'll be taking another semester off. I'm not quite done with the business that sent me away for the last couple of months."

Adora carefully set her cup down. "And when are you going to tell me what that business was?" Her voice grew quiet. "What were you looking for, Theo?"

"Looking for?"

"You were on a diving ship. Diving ships are known for one thing: finding things."

He shook his head. "I can't tell you, Adora, not yet. If you knew, you would be in danger."

Her eyes flickered. "Theo, does that mean you're in danger?"

After a moment, he nodded. "It seems that way."

Adora studied him, then reached out and touched his arm. "Please keep safe. If there is anything I can do to help, let me know."

Theo gave her hand a pat. "I will, Adora. I promise. When the time is right."

"And keep Cass safe." Before he could comment, she waved her hand at him. "If you're in danger, then I'm sure Cass is as well.

You're both involved in whatever is going on."

"I will, Adora. You can count on that." If something happened to Cass, then their best chance at saving humanity went with her. Theo stood. "I should go. I have a couple Mist samples I'm studying down in the lab."

Adora gave him a sad smile. "I don't have to remind you not to let Grandfather know about your experiments anymore."

His heart twinged at her words. "No. But I can tell you, he'd be fine with what I'm doing."

She glanced up curiously, but he merely kissed her on the cheek and left the room.

THE FOLLOWING DAY BROUGHT OUT THE SUN AND humidity. Theo wiped at his goggles before putting them on again while Cass gazed at the zipper.

"I've never seen one this close before." She walked around the brass-colored flyer, fingers trailing along the wing and side. "It's beautiful."

"I thought you'd like it—and a chance to get away from the manse for a bit." He placed his leather valise in the back. A small trip with the zipper shouldn't be too taxing on her.

"I feel much better now," she said quickly. "I almost feel like myself again."

"In that case, shall we get going?"

Cass pulled her goggles down over eager eyes. She wore her diving clothes, cleaned and pressed, with her tunic tucked into her corset, a pair of dark trousers, and calf-high boots. Theo wondered what Adora would think of Cass's ensemble. Adora liked fashion, and he doubted she would wear men's clothing.

But the functionality and adventurous look fit Cass.

Theo opened the door for Cass, then went around and climbed in on the other side. With a click, he started the zipper. The wings buzzed as they fluttered madly on either side of the cockpit. Theo eased up on the clutch and brought the zipper up about twenty feet from the landing pad, then turned it toward the left and started across the sky.

The city of Belhold lay below, a sprawling collection of narrow homes, cobblestone streets, and factories across two mountain peaks and numerous valleys.

"Wow." He heard Cass exclaim over the buzz of the wings.

He glanced over at her and grinned. "It's amazing, isn't it?" he shouted.

"Yes! We never took the *Daedalus* over Belhold, only toward the pier in the factory district. This view is amazing!"

Theo swerved the zipper toward the left and aimed for the western side of Belhold. Cass had introduced him to the joy of diving—it was his turn to show her the joy of flying.

Seconds later, however, his smile ebbed away. As they drew closer to the border, a feeling of unease spread across his chest. Barricades and signs were set up in the streets between run-down tenements. A block beyond lay the Mist, a greenish-grey fog spread between decrepit buildings and abandoned streets. Theo narrowed his eyes as a prickling erupted across his back. This was not where the Mist had been months ago. In fact—he glanced down again as he flew over the border—it was now a couple blocks into the city, much further than he'd predicted.

This was bad. Very bad.

He brought the zipper to a bare spot a mile to the east and landed. He turned off the engine, pushed his goggles back, and reached for his valise.

"Was that really the Mist edging into the city?" Cass said as she exited the zipper from the other side.

"Yes."

"It's risen that much?"

"It appears that way."

With each step they descended deeper into the slums, and Theo's apprehension grew. Where were all the people? Despite how far the Mist had risen, there should still be people living in these buildings. Hundreds, crowded together, dwelling one step away from the Mist's deadly edge.

"I know this place," Cass said, looking around as they headed along streets so narrow that if Theo held out his arms, he could touch both walls, blocking out all light except for high above.

He glanced at her. "You do?"

"Yes," her voice dropped. "This is near where I lost my parents."

Her words sent a sobering chill across his chest as the reality of the Purges hit him. This was probably what a dead zone looked like after a Purge: empty, silent, grave-like. Suddenly the sun high above didn't seem so friendly or cheerful.

A block later, they bypassed the wooden barricade made of thick planks. Just beyond the nearest building, the Mist hovered like water along the banks of a river, a rolling, living greenish-grey. Theo stopped and pulled out a gas-mask for himself and Cass from his leather valise. He had to check just how far the Mist had risen from the last bar he had placed before leaving on the *Daedalus*.

Cass took the mask without question and pulled it on. He was sure she was immune, but there was still something that hesitated inside of him. Better to be safe than sorry.

Masks in place, they walked down the street and into the Mist. The first thing he noticed was how thick and chilly the air became, rising up his legs and torso. The sun disappeared, leaving only a subtle orb behind.

He glanced back once to make sure Cass was behind him before continuing. If the buildings had seemed empty and quiet above the Mist, down here they appeared haunted, as if an apparition could appear any moment. Thoughts of Voxhollow entered his mind.

We won't be here long, just enough so I can get a measurement and a sample. The thought barely reassured him, but it did make him move faster. He could sense Cass's presence, following close. They drew further into the Mist until they reached the edge of the tenements. A long scorched line, five feet wide, spread along the ground from left to right as far as the eye could see. It was where the fires would have burned during a Purge, keeping the people inside the Mist and killing off any Turned who tried to venture back. For a moment, his mind flickered to Luron, burned so badly that half his body was now encased in metal. The one other person known to be immune to the Mist.

This burn line was recent, maybe a month old? He knew this because his measuring rod was further in. Theo stepped across the scorched ground, avoiding charred pieces of wood, and headed across the small open space. There. A thin pole stood in the soil, three feet high. He looked back, noting the edge of the Mist three blocks away, then back at the pole. The Mist had risen that much in a month.

His throat tightened. So much, so fast. What if Cass's blood didn't provide a solution? What if there was no cure for the Mist? What if—

No. Theo took in a deep breath. Thoughts like those weren't going to help. Right now he needed facts: numbers, details, data. Concrete evidence, not flighty what-ifs.

With that thought in mind, he placed his valise on the ground and began to pull out his notes and lab microscope. Time to get to work.

8

CASS WATCHED AS THEO RUMMAGED THROUGH HIS valise. Then she looked around at the gathered Mist drifting between old and familiar buildings like a morning vapor. Yes, she knew this place. Just being here brought back those early memories with startling clarity. Her heart felt heavy. She reached for the thin necklace around her neck and clutched the locket.

Could Theo be right? Was it possible that something inside her blood had prevented her from Turning? Or was it just a happenstance? Perhaps her mask had only slipped halfway across her face, still protecting her in some way? Or she had somehow breathed in a patch of untainted air?

Cass felt along the leather and metal that formed the gas-mask she wore. She breathed in the stale air, filtered by the two cylinder-shaped appendages. Her fingers hesitated. What if she took off her mask right now?

Her heart quickened. Could she do it?

Theo stood by the wooden rod sticking up from a patch of bare ground. He held a thin white rope and placed one end at the base of the rod, then started toward the edge of the Mist. Cass stepped back to make room for him, her hand still clutching her locket.

All it would take would be to loosen her mask and pull it down, and she would be assured of the truth. Her hand lingered along the band. But what if she Turned?

Was it worth the risk? What was she thinking?

But what if Theo was right? Shouldn't they make sure? He was placing a lot of confidence in his belief that she was immune.

She pulled at her locket again, lightly tugging the thin chain around her neck. Was it true?

Could something inside her save other lives?

Her fingers stopped. She stared at the wall ahead.

I have to know.

Before another thought could form, Cass loosened the strap of her mask. She pulled the mask down and let it settle beneath her chin. She took a breath. Cold, misty air entered her lungs, a contrast to the mustiness from her mask. Her heart thumped madly inside her chest, but she held on.

Another breath.

Images of Captain Gresley Turning filled her mind, bringing a weakness to her legs.

But she breathed in again. She wondered, how long did it take for the spores to dominate a person?

She took stock of her body. Everything felt normal except for fear pounding within her veins. No tingling, no loss of vision, nothing she could imagine would happen during a Turning. She took another breath.

More seconds ticked by, and with each one, and each breath, hope swelled within her. A sudden desire to laugh and dance and sing took hold of her. She didn't know how it was possible, but here she was, breathing inside the Mist. She pressed a fist to her heart and looked up at the sky. Whatever kept her alive could possibly help others as well. *Elaeros. Is this you? Did you do this?*

There was a shout from Theo. "Cass! What are you doing?"

Cass spun around to find Theo dashing toward her, a look of horror in his eyes.

"Theo! You're right! I can breathe! I can—"

He grabbed her by the shoulders. "What in the gales possessed you to do such a thing?"

The smile fled her face. "What do you mean?"

"You took off your mask! Why?"

"You said I was immune. So I wanted to see for myself."

"But what if I was wrong?" He was almost shaking her.

She yanked away from him. "You weren't wrong! I'm not Turning!"

"But I could have been!"

"I had to know for myself!"

They stared at each other, both breathing hard. Theo hadn't said anything about the possibility of being wrong. And he was thorough enough that something significant like this wouldn't have passed his notice. Why was he reacting this way?

He ran a hand through his hair. "I'm sorry. It's just when I saw you with your mask gone, it all came back—when I found you without it before. That awful feeling of waiting for you to Turn took over, and I reacted. I'm sorry, Cass."

She suddenly saw herself through Theo's eyes, the same way she'd watched Captain Gresley turn. Her growing ire deflated. "Theo." As an apology formed on her lips, she caught a movement to her right.

Theo must have seen it too. His head whipped around.

A tall, gangly Turned appeared at the corner of a three-story tenement a block away, barely visible in the thick Mist. Except for his movement, he appeared almost normal: no exposed bone, no decaying flesh, as if he had Turned recently.

Cass reached for her side only to realize she wasn't carrying her revolver. She quickly calculated the distance between where they stood and the edge of the Mist.

Theo must have been thinking the same thing. He grabbed his valise, then her hand, and whispered, "Run!"

Cass didn't hesitate. They fled between the abandoned tenements and along the dirt street. Two blocks away from where they could see a hint of blue sky, three more Turned appeared between them and the edge of the Mist, barring the way along the narrow street. Theo stuttered to a stop, his hand still gripping Cass's. A man, a woman, and—bile filled her throat—a child no older than five or six stood there, eyes glazed, standing unnaturally still.

"Elaeros," Theo breathed. "A child?"

Cass pulled him to the left and down a narrow alley. She knew this area—she knew where to run. They ran between dilapidated brick walls, sagging wooden structures, and trash still left from a previous Purge. They could only see about ten feet ahead. For a brief moment, Cass thought how strange it felt to be running in the fog without her mask on.

At the corner, she led them out onto another dirt street and headed for the edge of the Mist. No Turned blocked their path this time. They ran out into untainted air. Theo ripped off his mask, fell to his knees, and retched across the dirt road.

Cass knelt next to him. She'd seen children driven into the Mist during a Purge, so she knew they Turned. But apparently this was Theo's first time.

"I can't believe that," he said weakly as he wiped his mouth. Then he noticed the foul liquid pooling in the dirt. "I'm sorry, Cass."

"It's not the first time I've seen vomit," she replied matter-of-factly.

"And children?"

"I've seen them, too."

Theo stumbled to his feet. Cass picked up his valise and began to head through the tenements toward the wooden barricade ahead. She was starting to feel the exertion of being out after her recent illness, and Theo didn't seem to be in a mind to continue his studies.

"Wait." She turned toward his voice and realized he hadn't moved. "I can't go, not yet." Behind him, at Mist's edge, the handful of Turned they had run into now stood along the border, watching them. "I still need spore samples."

Cass peered at the Turned again. "Then we better collect them somewhere else."

Theo followed her glance. "You're right," he said reluctantly, then rebounded. "We'll fly to another spot, and I can measure how much the Mist has swelled and retrieve a fresh sample there."

"Are you sure?"

His face tightened. "After all we've seen, I can't stop now, Cass. The Mist, the Purges, the echelons who are responsible for turning human beings—even children—into lifeless monsters. It needs to end."

She lifted an eyebrow at his slang use of echelon.

"Will you help me?"

There was a new strength in his voice and an even firmer determination to see this through to the end. Fresh energy filled her body. She could keep going. She stared into his dark eyes and nodded. "Yes, I will."

9

"THIS WAS JUST DELIVERED FOR YOU, MASTER THEO. The messenger said it is urgent."

Theo took the proffered note from Hannah. He and Cass had landed and just entered the manse. "Did the messenger say who it is from?"

"Yes. The House of Lords. There is a meeting tonight and your presence is requested."

His fingers tightened around the note. He hadn't been in contact with the House of Lords since his journey with the *Daedalus*. Not that he'd missed much. They seemed fine with making unilateral decisions without him, like placing Voxhollow in a no-fly zone.

He turned to Cass behind him. "I'm afraid I have a meeting this evening. Will you be alright by yourself?"

"Of course I will." She pulled her goggles from her head. "I'm actually feeling a bit tired, so I may spend time in my room anyway."

Theo nodded. "Good idea."

Hannah was asking Cass if she had eaten as Theo entered his study and shut the door. He let out a long breath as he collapsed in the chair behind his desk. He held the note for a moment before opening it. The words were formal and direct: *Board meeting at six. Your presence required.*

Theo put the note down and thrummed his fingers along the desk. Many people would give everything they had to sit on the council of the Five Families—some had even tried—but it was an inherited position, one he knew he should be thankful for. But right now it felt like a burden. No, more than that. Like chains. The more he discovered, the more removed he felt from the rest of the Families. His goals were different, his view of the world was different. He was different.

But his position also gave him a rare opportunity to change the world. He could almost hear Cass's voice chastising him for not being grateful for what he had. He smirked. What would the meeting be like if someone like her attended?

His thoughts turned to her and that morning. He still couldn't believe she had removed her mask. He leaned across his desk and placed his head in his hand. So reckless. And curious. And independent.

He wouldn't have her any other way.

He sat up and stared at the note again. He would go and start using the position he had been given to do what was right.

A CHILL HUNG OVER THE MEETING ROOM DESPITE the warm evening outside. Two gaslit chandeliers presided over the long table surrounded by leatherback chairs. The deep-red velvet curtains were pulled shut. Most of the houses were present, along with their heirs. Titus Kingsford sat at the head of the table with his twin sons behind him. Margaret Etherington was on Theo's right with her daughter behind her. Reynard

Atwood was on the left, one of the few Families that lived away from Belhold. Charity stood in the shadows near him and gave Theo a small wave. He nodded in her direction as he went to take the seat once occupied by his grandfather. He would be sure to thank her for helping him procure the flight papers last minute that helped the *Daedalus* reach Voxhollow.

The *Daedalus.*

His chest tightened as he sat down. He still hadn't found out what happened that day. But he was sure he knew what family had ordered Luron—

He frowned as he looked around for Salomon Staggs. In his stead sat his son William. He looked the same as always, his boyishly handsome face holding a slightly bored expression.

"Where's your father?" Theo asked.

William glanced at him as if he just now was aware of Theo's presence. "Away on House of Lords' business. Where have you been?"

"Also away on business of a personal matter."

William gave him a sardonic grin. "I hope your personal matter was important enough to lose your position as head of the class."

For a moment, regret filled Theo's heart. More than anything, he loved the academic life. Regret faded as firm conviction took its place—what he was doing was much more important. "It was."

William seemed taken aback but replied airily, "Oh, well, you've not been missed."

If that was supposed to hurt his feelings, William had a long way to go. Theo waited for the meeting to come to order.

Titus Kingsford looked his way from across the table. "Theodore Winchester." The room grew quiet. "So you have chosen to grace us with your presence."

Theo met his gaze. "I'm afraid I've been away for the last couple months for personal reasons."

"And you didn't seem to feel it was important to inform us of your absence?"

"I wasn't under the impression that my private affairs were the business of the House of Lords," he replied.

"When it takes you away for weeks at a time, causing you to miss these meetings, then it is our business. Five votes, one for each Family. That is how things are run."

Theo placed his hands on the table. "Then let me ask you something. When was a no-flight zone placed along the western mountains? I know it happened before I left. If my vote is so important that you demand to know my personal business, then I wish to know why the house of Winchester was not part of that vote. And why was it put in place?"

"The decision was made during the transition of your place here."

"The transition of me taking over my grandfather's seat happened the moment he passed away."

Titus's tone was supercilious. "We didn't want to burden you during your time of grief."

"Or you wanted to secure that area without my vote," Theo shot back. "So to my other question, why?"

"Because it is a dangerous place," Margaret Etherington interrupted. "There was an accident near the area, and we were informed that there are strange Turned roving that part of the country. It is our responsibility to keep people safe. So"—she adjusted her monocle with a haughty stare—"we chose to make that section of the western mountains off limits."

"Why now?" Theo persisted. He looked around at the others. "Has there never been an expedition to the area before?"

Titus Kingsford, Margaret Etherington, and Reynard Atwood exchanged glances while the Staggs scion merely appeared puzzled.

Reynard cleared his throat. "There have been small expeditions from time to time along the western mountains. The area was picked clean right after the war, and nothing of value has been found since. Hardly a ship goes there now. But recently there has been more traffic, and since there is nothing but ruins, we chose to vote the best way possible to keep people safe."

Reynard seemed to genuinely believe his words. Could that mean that the other Families didn't know about the Staggs's western expedition that had cost the *Daedalus* their captain? Theo wasn't convinced about that, but this was not the place to argue.

Theo inclined his head. "I understand. My desire is to honor the seat my family has held at this table for almost two hundred years. I will make sure to be present when I am called; therefore I ask that decisions are not made without the Winchester vote."

Reynard spoke up. "Then we will do our part to include you. Forgive our discourtesy."

"Next." Titus brought the attention of the room back on him. "We need to discuss the Mist. The last Purge wasn't enough to secure Belhold or Tyromourne. Both are seeing rising panic in the lower levels, and the people there are taking flight before the bluecoats can arrive and deal with them. Those along the middle rings are starting to complain about the surge in population, theft, and violence."

William snorted. "We should round up the whole lot of them and shove them in the Mist with one massive Purge. They only take up useful space and resources."

"They're humans," Reynard Atwood said quietly.

"Not when we Purge them," Margaret retorted. "They're more like vermin before they're Turned anyway."

Theo's hand curled in his lap. The image of the small Turned child came to mind. "Maybe instead of Purges," he said with an edge to his voice, "we should be focusing on dealing with the Mist."

Reynard nodded. "Perhaps you are right—" he began, but Titus cut him off.

"We pursued that venue a long time ago. It was not a viable option."

What? Theo fought to control his anger. "I've never heard of this. Why is it not a viable option?"

Titus looked sharply at Theo. "Because there is no cure. Fire is the best way to eradicate the Mist. We tried. We burned the Mist in the valleys, but by the time one area was cleared, the Mist had already moved back into the others. And the spores themselves work too fast on the human body."

"So over two hundred years, we've discovered nothing."

"Tread carefully, Winchester. For two hundred years our Families have held humanity together. And it's only until recently that we believed the Mist affected everyone."

"Luron." *And Cass,* Theo thought to himself.

"Yes." Titus said and turned his attention to William. "Has your father discovered the reason for Luron's unusual trait? Does he know yet if it is possible to produce more like Luron without involving the Mist?"

William crossed his arms and leaned back in his chair. "No. Which is another reason to Purge the entire bottom district. We would be getting rid of surplus population and might find more who don't Turn in the Mist."

"Why don't we discover why he doesn't Turn and use that instead?" Theo said.

"Why would we do that when we can simply use him?"

Theo was disgusted. "Because we could possibly save all of humanity?"

"We're already saving people. Us. Why would we want to keep those who do nothing but steal, squat in squalor, and defile the lives of civilized people?"

"Have you actually met the people you're talking about?"

William's eyes flashed. "I have. Even had one draw a knife on me. Couldn't reason with him."

Theo leaned toward William, voice rising. "Perhaps he was driven to do what he did by hunger and need—"

"Enough!" Titus glared at Theo. "I already answered your question. And yet you continue to push the topic. There is no stopping the Mist. There is only adaptation. Your grandfather knew this."

"You have a lot to learn, young man," Margaret Etherington added. "About your place and the place of others. Choose carefully with whom you want to associate." Her daughter nodded behind her.

Theo stared at the people around the table. These were the leaders of the world, the protectors of humanity. But they weren't interested in protecting anyone but themselves. Even worse, they didn't consider those below them as humans. No wonder the Purges continued. And with the Mist rising, more Purges would happen.

Theo sat, tense, as Titus shared the housing situation in Tyromourne and how the rapidly rising Mist had affected that area. Words. Just words. That's all they were.

But he wouldn't use just words. He glanced again at Reynard, then at Charity standing behind him. Perhaps they could be allies. At least maybe Charity. He had a feeling Reynard had become passive a long time ago.

He would contact Professor Hawkins at the university. Surely the professor would help him this time, since he was coming with substantial hope.

And he would continue to speak up at these meetings, despite the peril. He was the only one who could. Until they stopped him. Permanently, one way or another.

As the meeting drew to a close and Theo stood up, Charity Atwood made her way around the table. She looked lovely, a cream-colored gown accentuating her lean curves and rich dark skin. "Theodore, it is good to see you," she said with a smile.

"Same to you."

She reached out her hands to clasp his. "I hope you can visit me again in Decadenn."

He stiffened at her touch until he felt a slip of paper pressed into his hands. "Of course. Perhaps I can bring my sister Adora. Have you met her?" He could feel William's eyes on him.

"No, I have not had the pleasure." She casually let go of his hands.

"You two have a lot in common. Your minds think alike."

"Then I would very much like to meet your sister. Until then." She gave him a small bow, then went back to her father, who was currently speaking with Titus.

Theo left the meeting room and strode down the hall as the sun sank below the horizon outside the windows. Once he was sure he was alone, he paused for a moment to glance at the note.

There was only once sentence, written in strong curved letters.

They are coming for you.

10

THEO STUFFED THE NOTE INTO HIS INNER POCKET and headed outside. As he prepped his zipper for flight, his mind kept mulling over the message. Who? The House of Lords? Were Titus's words a hidden threat?

He stared at his zipper, then double-checked everything. Nothing out of place, damaged, or sabotaged. As far as he could tell, there would be no "accident" like what had happened to his parents.

Theo climbed in and started the motor. The wings on either side of the cockpit began to whirr, and he pulled back on the throttle. The zipper lifted into the air as streaks of red and purple spread across the evening sky.

The vagueness of the note indicated Charity was sure he would know to whom it alluded. Which meant the House of Lords. Was the meeting tonight to make sure he was in Belhold? Then why didn't they come after him at the meeting?

Maybe not everyone was in on it.

Were the Atwoods allies?

Adora met Theo at the door as he entered through the back after securing the zipper.

"Salomon Staggs is here to see you along with a couple of

bluecoats," she said with a puzzled look on her face. "And a very strange man."

He halted. "Describe this strange man."

"He's wearing a gold mask, with slits for his eyes and mouth," she said. Then added, "He's dressed like a gentleman."

Luron.

Adora looked at him questioningly. "Wasn't Salomon supposed to be at the House of Lords meeting with you?"

"He wasn't there." Theo's mind raced as he removed his coat and hat and handed them to Hannah, who was waiting beside Adora. William had said his father was away on House of Lords' business. "Did he say why he's here?"

"No. It seems odd. Did something happen?"

So it had come to this. Either Salomon was acting alone, or the House of Lords was determined to silence him. There was no doubt Salomon was involved—Salomon was the only one who could have sent Luron after him in Voxhollow. What might happen to Adora . . . or Aunt Maude? Theo glanced at his sister's troubled face.

He needed to tell her the truth, at least part of it. "Adora, on his deathbed, Grandfather disclosed a family secret." He took in a deep breath. "There's been a cure for the Mist. Our family has had it for years." She gasped. He took her hands and looked into her eyes. "That's what I've been doing for the last two months, retrieving that cure."

"You can't be serious." Her voice was barely audible.

"I am. Long have I suspected the House of Lords did not want a cure, and tonight's meeting confirmed that. They even sent someone to stop me during the trip to Voxhollow. Like they stopped Father and Mother."

Her eyes widened in disbelief. "You mean their accident wasn't an accident?" He could see her mind whirring as he nodded. Her face and tone grew hard. "Then if Salomon is here for you, you shouldn't see him. You need to go, now. I'll tell him you left on a trip again. Which you are."

Theo tightened his hold on her hands. "Adora, you don't understand. I know you can handle Salomon. It's the other. He's the one who tried to kill us in Voxhollow."

"You didn't tell me that when you arrived."

"Because I didn't want to scare you."

She drew herself straight. "I'm not a little girl, Theo. I can handle the truth. All of it. You need to let me help you."

For one hot moment he wanted to march down the hallway and confront Salomon Staggs, consequences be hanged.

Adora shook her head. "I know what you're thinking. Don't do it. You said you were looking for a cure. Did you find something?"

"Yes, I believe so."

"Then you need to go, and keep that knowledge safe. The world very well might be depending on you."

"But, Adora—"

She put a hand to his mouth. "Hush, brother. Now go."

Adora was right. He had to allow her to help him. "Alright. I'll get Cass, and we'll leave now." He wanted to tell her that there was a chance, a *real chance*, that they could be on the brink of changing the world. But the more she knew, the more she would be in danger.

She smiled at him. "Don't worry, I can take care of Salomon Staggs. And I've already been taking care of myself and Aunt Maude while you were away." She poked him in the chest. "You make sure you take care of Cass. I like her. She's good for you." Adora started to leave, then turned. "I'll be at church on Sunday. Find a way to meet me, and I'll relay any information I discover tonight. In the meantime, you stay safe."

"I will. See you Sunday." He wasn't sure yet how he would find her at church without being noticed, but he had two days to figure that out. Right now, he needed to disappear.

While Adora headed down the hall, Theo made his way silently up the staircase. He only had minutes to get himself and Cass away. Adora was good at conversation, but he wasn't going to take any chances that Salomon might see through her bluff.

At the top, he spotted Cass emerging from the library, still dressed in her *Daedalus* apparel.

"We need to go," he said abruptly.

Instead of asking questions, she nodded. She followed him along the hall to his room where he had stored the gliders. Gas lamps along the hall flickered as night took hold of the manse. The packs were next to his dresser where he had left them when they first arrived. He snatched one and held the other out to Cass. She took it and swung it on. Next, he opened the small wooden box on the top and pulled a handful of sterlings out and stuffed them in his front pocket.

"I'll warn you, I've never glided at night," Cass whispered as they headed toward the back of the manse. "It's not considered safe. But I'm assuming it's our only option."

"Yes. The bluecoats are here. And the zipper would take too long to prep and makes too much noise. Adora is stalling for us and will tell Salomon Staggs I'm away again. I want to make sure there is as much truth to her statement as possible."

"Staggs? The Five Families' Staggs?"

"Yes, the same one who sent Luron after us."

Quietly they took the stairs in the rear and made it to the back door.

The air was clear and warm, with a slight breeze. Stars twinkled above, and a half moon shone over the small yard that lined the landing pad for the zipper. Cass was already equipping her glider, tugging on the straps and making sure everything was secure.

Theo stepped into his own loops. What would they do when they reached the surface? Where would they land? Would they land, or would they crash to their deaths?

What in the Mist am I doing? He stared at the strap in his hand. *This is madness.* He had half a mind again to turn around and demand answers from Salomon Staggs. But if something happened to him, Cass would have no one. And the secret that lay within her blood would die away.

No.

He finished his own straps. He was doing this for her. He was the only one who knew that Cass was able to walk in the Mist. That she was possibly humanity's hope.

"I'm ready," Cass told him.

"So am I."

They headed toward the edge of the sky island. He took in a deep breath and let it out slowly. At least they didn't need their gas-masks.

At the edge, they stopped. Cass looked down. He noted her pensive expression as she studied the city of Belhold below. "Let's not use our goggles," she suggested. "It will obscure our vision slightly, and we are going to need to see as much as we can in the dark."

Theo nodded.

"I say we should head west, toward the factories. More places to land, less people. And there are usually small storerooms that we might find refuge in tonight."

Again, Theo nodded. He would defer to whatever Cass said. She was the one with more knowledge in this area.

She pulled on the cord and let her glider spread out behind her. "This is going to be quite the experience."

Before Theo could respond, Cass stepped off the ledge. A moment later, she sailed up as she caught the breeze. Theo pulled on his own cord. Once she was a safe enough distance away, he stepped off the same ledge.

Below him, the city of Belhold twinkled like a thousand stars. A frightening thrill soared through him as he caught the wind and moved forward. So different than gliding during the day.

And so beautiful.

He could barely see Cass ahead—the only parts visible were her canvas wings, illuminated by the dim moonlight. She ascended for a moment, then dipped down and started westward. Her flight pattern reminded him of a hawk: graceful, serene, and deadly.

The cityscape changed as they approached the factory district of Belhold. Instead of a scattering of small twinkling lamps inside of homes, large lights appeared in a set pattern, illuminating the way for airships and third-shift factory workers. Beyond the factories, faint moonlight flickered off the surface of the Mist.

Cass angled toward a long walkway of metal that connected the airship pier to the factories. Theo followed, the darkness starting to get to him. Just as she approached, she brought up her glider and came to a landing. Theo came up behind her, but miscalculated the distance and stalled too soon. He fell the extra two feet and slammed his knees into the metal grates.

"Are you alright?" Cass whispered as her glider slipped into her pack.

"Yes," he said through tight lips, although he could already feel blood seeping through one pant leg. He hadn't broken or sprained anything, and for that he was grateful. He slowly stood and stowed away his glider. They were here now, and temporarily away from danger. They both looked around at the belching factories, smog-filled air, and endless walkways and gangplanks. Theo's mind stuttered. He wasn't sure where they should go or what to do next. This place was like nothing he'd ever seen.

As if hearing his thoughts, Cass turned to him and grinned. "Welcome to my world."

11

"FIRST THINGS FIRST," CASS SAID. "WE NEED TO FIND a spot to stow our gliders. It might even be a place where we can stay for the night."

She looked around. Fortunately, they had landed on a familiar gangplank. A textile factory stood nearby, a five-story brick building built into the hillside and connected to the walkway.

"This way," she said. A handful of gas lamps lighted their path as they scurried along the metal planks, bypassing another factory, a long metal building with the smell of coal clinging to the air.

"Are we going to stay in the Steelhold district?" Theo asked minutes later.

"Yes. It's too dark tonight to find another place. You have to be careful on the streets. There's no such thing as abandoned houses or buildings. Sometimes you'll get lucky after a Purge and the bluecoats have cleared out a place. And even then, the Mist is always rising. There was always a chance of waking up to the Mist outside your door."

"Especially now with how fast the Mist is moving."

"That's true." How many people died in their sleep because the Mist took them during the night? Cass shuddered at the thought. No, they would stay here tonight, and scout out a new place tomorrow or the next day.

As they neared the textile plant, Cass paused for a moment on the metal walkway that served as the main thoroughfare along the labyrinth of factories spread across the Steelhold district. She looked down into the dark valley and stilled. Was that the Mist?

"What is it?"

Cass frowned. "I've never seen the Mist here before. It's always been beyond the Yorke River."

Theo looked over the side, then shook his head. "We'll need to be careful."

Cass took the stairway at the corner and headed down into the darkness. The textile factory consisted of a main floor, then offices, then dorms for the women who worked there. Years ago, she'd tried to find work there herself, but the factory had been full. However, she had discovered a rarely used storage room right off the main floor. It became one of the many spots she would frequent when she needed a place to stay.

It would work perfectly tonight, as long as it was still vacant. She hoped so.

They reached the bottom of the steps. Hardly any light trickled down along this area. Using her memory, Cass followed the foundation, turned the corner, and found the small wooden door, a barely visible square amongst the bricks. Weeds and brush grew along the side of the building, scraping her arms as she walked by. Once she reached the door, she turned the handle and tugged, but the door wouldn't budge.

"Here, let me," Theo whispered. "It's catching on the ground." Cass stepped back, letting Theo by. She glanced again at the Mist as Theo worked the door. It was at least thirty feet away if not farther. They should be safe for now. He pulled until finally there was an opening big enough for them to squeeze through.

"I'll go first," she said quietly, "since I'm familiar with the storage area." Theo stepped away and she entered the room. There was a hiss as something dashed across the dirt floor. Cass froze until her mind caught up with her.

It was only a cat. The factory kept them around to keep the rats out.

She let out a huge breath and felt along the room. A couple broken wooden crates and old metal factory frames lined the walls, leaving about a six-foot space. Cass worked the straps of her glider, her eyes slowly adjusting to the faint light coming in through the door. She heaved off her pack and placed it against the wall, then sank down to the floor, her back against one of the crates. She heard Theo doing the same thing, and a moment later, he sat down beside her. They both breathed in the darkness, taking in a moment of quiet and safety.

"So how bad is your knee?" Cass asked.

"I scraped it and there will be a bruise."

She looked over at him. She could see the profile of his face. "Should we do something about it? Like bandage it up?"

"I don't think we can until morning."

He was right. There was hardly any light.

They both sat silently for a while. Glittery yellow eyes peered at them from the other side of the room. "So what happened?" Cass asked as she pulled her legs up to her chest and wrapped her arms around them. "You said something about bluecoats and the Staggs family."

She heard Theo shift beside her. "I'm not sure about all the details. But what I do know is after the board meeting tonight, Charity Atwood gave me a note that said they were coming for me."

"Who exactly?"

"I know the Staggs family is one. I suspect a few of the other Families of the House of Lords as well."

She tried to see his face, but the light was too dim. "Why?"

"Power. They want to stay in power." His voice was tight. "The Mist gives them authority over the population: who lives, who dies, who is elevated, and who is destroyed. They killed my parents because their search might have diminished the power of the House of Lords."

"And now they are going after you."

"I'm sure of it. Because I am following in my father's footsteps."

"I don't understand. They're supposed to be taking care of people. Why wouldn't they want a cure? People would be grateful to them."

"Remember what I said? Power. The power to control people."

It sounded senseless to Cass. "And who will they control when the Mist finally covers everything and everyone is Turned?"

"Exactly. But I don't think they care. Some of them don't even consider those below them as human."

Her heart constricted. "Like me."

"Yes," came the quiet reply.

Heat flushed through her. The words *street rat* echoed in her mind.

"But you know I don't think like that," Theo went on. "And others in that room tonight didn't, either. We may have some allies."

"But still . . ."

"I think it's ironic that out of everyone Elaeros could have gifted with an immunity to the Mist, it happens to be a young-woman-off-the-streets-turned-diver."

She turned toward him. "You think Elaeros gave me this?"

"Yes."

There was such confidence in his voice that it washed away the questions at the edge of her mind. Elaeros. Not some heir of the House of Lords or even one of the people along the middle rings of Belhold. Elaeros gave this ability to her.

She wondered what Captain Gresley would have thought. No, she knew. He would believe the same thing. That she was meant to have this. And if so, she would make sure she did something good with it.

Exhaustion hit her and she let out a yawn. She curled nearer to Theo for warmth and closed her eyes. She'd never been close to anyone. Definitely not on the streets where she was constantly alone. And on the *Daedalus* she'd bunked away from the rest of the crew.

He stiffened next to her, but she didn't care. "You're not too bad for an echelon," she said, followed by another yawn and closed her eyes. Sleep drew her.

Theo laughed and relaxed. "And you're not too bad for a diver."

She smiled with her eyes shut. He had a scent to him, of fresh air and cloves. Comforting. Safe. The darkness and warmth beckoned her forward until her head bobbed and she drifted away with the feel of his wool sweater beneath her cheek.

THE MUFFLED SOUND OF VOICES AND WARM LIGHT brought Cass around. She blinked at the partially opened door as she awoke.

A bell began to ring outside, signaling the start of the workday.

At the sound, Theo jerked up abruptly. His dark eyes came to focus on her, and then he began to twist his body one way, then the other. "I'm stiff."

Cass crawled away and stood. She was used to sleeping on the ground, in hammocks, or even curled up on balconies.

"How's your knee?" she asked.

Theo looked down. There was a tear along his trousers. He rolled the pant leg up, exposing a patch of crusted blood and a large purple bruise.

"That looks terrible."

Theo shrugged and rolled his pant leg back down. "Just a scratch and bruise, but nothing more." He stood up and gave his leg a shake. "Still functional."

"So what's next?"

"Good question. I was able to grab a handful of sterlings, so we have some money, but not much. Adora said she would meet me on Sunday to let me know what she found out. I had planned to visit the university and talk to one of my professors about you. I'm hoping he might know someone who is able to help us."

"This is the person you said you can trust."

"I believe so. I've talked to him before about my findings and thoughts. The sooner I can get to him, the better."

Thunder rumbled outside as he spoke.

"Alright," Cass said. "Let's stow our gliders here behind these crates. They should be safe for the time being."

Theo pulled out the wad of sterlings while Cass lifted her glider and carried it over to the dark corner between the crates. She glanced over at him as she tucked the glider into the gap. "What are you thinking about?"

"How to take care of our needs," he said without looking up.

"What do you mean?"

He held up the money. "There's not enough for food and room at an inn."

Cass thought quickly. "I have an idea. You go to the university while I find us food and scout out a couple places for us to stay. In fact"—she eyed him—"the streets are the best place for us to disappear. But that means you're going to have to dress like a scrounger."

He didn't even blink. "That's fine. But no stealing." He held out the sterlings to her.

Cass paused. "Did you think I was going to steal? Do you think I'm a thief?"

"I didn't mean that."

Cass sighed. "But you're right. It's not how I was brought up. No matter how hard it got, my father always found some work in order to buy food. But for a girl my age on the streets, there was one type of work I swore I would never do. Sometimes it came down to that or stealing. I chose the lesser evil."

Theo reddened. "Cass, I'm sorry. I didn't mean—"

Cass waved him off. "Life on the streets is hard. Ironically, the ones who are usually caught in the Purges are those trying to live a decent life, no matter their circumstances. Families, lower-level factory workers, refugees, and others who just can't afford to live along the higher tiers of Belhold."

Theo's lips were pressed tightly together. No wonder he didn't know—hardly any echelons understood the life of those along the borders. And apparently she didn't really understand the propriety of his class. They both still had a lot to learn about the other.

"You trust me with your money?"

Theo came out of his reverie. "Yes, Cass, I do. Buy whatever we need. And if you need more, I'll find a way to procure it."

She took the sterlings. There were more than she had seen in a lifetime. "I think this will be more than enough." The type of clothes he would need wouldn't be found in a shop. But she could probably convince someone to part with a jacket or old sweater. That is, if anyone was left from the Purges by the dead zone. The thought made her stomach constrict as she tucked the sterlings into her corset.

More thunder rumbled, and a couple heavy raindrops splatted across the dirt beyond the door.

"Well, one nice thing about this storm," Theo observed dryly, "it should cover my approach to the university. Everyone will be busy scurrying across the grounds with their heads bowed."

Cass grasped the sleeve of his coat. "Be careful, Theo."

He looked down at her, and his face softened. "I will. I should be back here sometime late afternoon or evening."

She nodded and slowly let go of his arm. She'd grown used to his presence. Theo was like a companion to her. A friend. And she didn't want to lose him. "I'll have everything we need when you get back." Fat raindrops sounded outside and she made a face. "But I think I'll wait until the rain lets up."

"Good idea." Then he left the storage area in a run, covering his head with his arms. The rain would also conceal their comings and goings from the factory and give her time to find them a better place to hide. Theo disappeared, and Cass sat down just inside the entryway and watched the heavens open up.

12

TWENTY MINUTES LATER, AND THOROUGHLY drenched, Theo reached the edge of the Steelhold district and hailed a cab. He gave the driver the address to the university then climbed into the back. The steam-powered vehicle took off with a lurch and started for the next hill. The rain tapered down to a drizzle, and Theo watched warehouses and brick buildings change to long narrow two-story homes, built next to each other. Other vehicles drove by, and a zipper flew overhead.

The cab entered the first valley, then started chugging its way up another hill, bypassing small shops and more homes. Just as they crested the top, the towers of Browning came into view. Sand-colored buildings filled the skyscape, with spires and curved windows. Grey-colored tiles covered the multiple roofs, and a scarlet banner hung limp in the rain from the topmost tower.

The prestigious university had occupied this hill in Belhold since before the Plague Wars and the world changed. Like an edifice to remind people that knowledge was always there to guide. That only worked if knowledge wasn't twisted or hidden away, Theo thought as the cab pulled up to the tall metal gates that marked the entrance.

He climbed out, handed the driver a sterling, then headed for the gates. Given the time, classes would be out soon, which meant students would be everywhere. The rain started again. He glanced up at the rumbling clouds and let out a sigh of relief. The storm would help mask his entrance.

The university clock chimed across the campus. A minute later, the building doors opened, and young men dressed in long dark robes with arms full of books or carrying valises crossed the grounds and made their way to another class or the library, their heads down to avoid the rain. They passed by Theo without making eye contact as he hurried toward to the smaller building to the east, where the faculty had their offices. Just as he approached the thick wooden door, William Staggs came out. Theo stopped, and he and William stared at each other, the rain falling on their heads.

His heart leapt into his throat. Gales, what should he do? The one person he didn't want to see was now standing before him.

"So you're finally returning," William said with a mocking air as he brushed past Theo.

Theo glanced back. Would William tell his father he saw him here at the university? He noticed a lone figure standing at the corner of the science building. The man's stature, and the way he was watching everything around the courtyard, made Theo quickly enter the administrative building. The door shut with a soft thud. Had he put himself back in danger by coming here?

He headed down the hallway. He had no choice. He needed help. Someone with medical knowledge. Someone who could decipher Cass's unique physiology.

Just as he reached Professor Hawkins office, the professor appeared around the corner, his white wispy hair as curly as ever. Theo glanced to the left and right, then lifted his hand in greeting. Professor Hawkins spotted him and hurried toward the office.

"Master Theo, what are you doing here?" He pulled out a bronze key while balancing a stack of papers with his other hand.

"I needed to see you."

Professor Hawkins shot him a glance. "You haven't been to Browning in months. I would have thought something happened to you if not for the memo stating you were taking a semester off."

"I needed some personal time after my grandfather's death."

Professor Hawkins swung the door open. "Understandable. But we are now in a new semester. Are you taking more time off?"

"Yes."

The older man let out a sigh as he motioned for Theo to enter. "And does this have something to do with the Mist?"

Theo's gut tightened. Was Professor Hawkins going to tell him he was wasting his time again? "Please, Professor, hear what I have to say."

Professor Hawkins let out another sigh. "I can do that much. Take a seat."

The office smelled as it always did, with a hint of pipe smoke, vanilla, and wood. A massive oak desk sat in front of a window from which Theo could see across the campus square. Bookcases lined the walls on either side, and an old, faded rug lay across the stone floor. Theo took the chair in front of the desk while Professor Hawkins laid his stack of papers down and out of the way.

"Alright," he said as he settled into his own chair and steepled his fingers together. "I'm listening."

Theo took a deep breath. He needed to trust someone, someone besides his family and Cass. It was hard to release the secrets he had kept close to his heart for the last few months, but it was time. This undertaking would require many people. So starting with the night his grandfather revealed their family secret, Theo began his story.

Professor Hawkins's frowned deepened as each minute passed until he finally stood up and walked over to the window behind his desk. After Theo finished, the office filled with silence. Was the professor going to believe him or turn him out like last time?

"I never wanted to involve you," Professor Hawkins finally said quietly, so quietly that Theo could barely hear him. "After your father died, I swore that no one else would be part of this." He shook his head and turned. "But you have information we need. And a possible cure with the young woman."

"What are you talking about?"

"There *is* a group that's been working on a cure, for as long as the Mist has filled our valleys. But we've been working in secret. I am a history professor by trade, but behind the scenes, I'm a researcher. And I'm not the only one. There are a handful of us, some part of the Alchemy Society, some within the universities, and even a couple of merchants who help with expenses. Your father was also part of our group, until his untimely demise. That's when we realized there might be a leak, and we almost completely shut down our work, fearing that the House of Lords had found out about us."

"But you told me to let things be, that this was the way of the world." Theo vividly remembered that conversation from less than a year ago when he'd first approached the professor.

Professor Hawkins inclined his head in acknowledgment. "Yes. You have no idea how much I wanted to bring you into our group. I wasn't lying when I said you are one of the brightest young men I've had the privilege of teaching. Your relentless search for the truth and keen desire for understanding were unparalleled. But I couldn't risk it. Not after the death of your parents. Not when the House of Lords was tracking down anyone who was doing research. Why do you think your grandfather was so intent on keeping you away from the Mist? As a member of the House of Lords, he knew what would happen to those who meddled with the desires of that group. I dare say he knew or at least suspected what happened to his son. And despite his own weaknesses, he didn't want to see that happen to you."

"Yes, that is true," Theo assented, thinking back to his grandfather's dying words.

"But if what you told me is true, things are different now. They're already after you. And more importantly, you may have the one thing that they never wanted you to find: a possible cure." Professor Hawkins sat down again and placed his hands on his desk. "Tell me more about this young woman. This Cass."

Theo described what happened in Voxhollow, his discovery of Cass without her mask on, how she hadn't Turned. And how a couple days ago, the same thing happened.

"Interesting, very interesting." Professor Hawkins tugged on his chin. "Here is what we know of the spores so far: Unlike most spores that are repelled through the skin and mucus systems, the Mist spores travel along the bloodstream and spread through the body until they take hold of the person."

"How did you discover that?"

The professor smiled wryly. "There has been a lot of time to perform studies over two hundred years. But there has never been someone whose very blood blocked the spores. Different researchers have tried other methods to stop it, but so far nothing has worked."

Professor Hawkins paused and then continued, "We're a handful of scientists who have been working with very little funding and in secret. We've never had the resources of the House of Lords or the Alchemy Society. Our progress has been very slow. Perhaps there have been others with this apparent blood immunity, but we never knew. And we still wouldn't know if you hadn't brought Cass to our attention." He let out a long breath. "You and your family have paid a heavy price in order to help us. And we are grateful for that. With Cass's blood, we might be able to replicate what's inside of her and share it with others."

"That doesn't solve the problem of the Mist," Theo pointed out.

"No, at least not that we know of. But it will give us a chance to study the Mist more intensely without fear of Turning. Or it might reveal a component we can exploit. It's even possible that instead of preventing the spores from traveling through her body, your young friend Cass is able to obliterate them completely."

"So what do we do next?" Theo asked.

The professor looked at him. "We will need a sample of Cass's blood."

"A sample? Do I bring her here?"

Professor Hawkins shook his head. "No, too risky. The university is being watched."

"I noticed."

"Instead, I'll have you take a sample and bring it back to me, at my residence."

"How do I take a sample?" Theo narrowed his eyes. "Not bloodletting, right?"

"No, no, that's barbaric. We have a new way of retrieving blood. Stay here, and I'll go see if we have the proper tools in the labs."

Theo watched Professor Hawkins leave, then wandered over to the seat in front of the desk. A clock ticked quietly somewhere in the office as the rain tapered off outside. The silence felt soothing, and Theo found his eyes growing heavy. He yawned and rubbed his face.

Professor Hawkins came back twenty minutes later with a small black leather bag. He placed the valise on top of the desk and opened it. Inside were a couple of miniature glass vials, a glass syringe, tiny needles, and a long rubber tube. Definitely not the tools Theo had seen for bloodletting. He leaned closer. "So how does this work?"

"Simple." Professor Hawkins went through the process, showing Theo how to collect the blood sample. Theo watched, fascinated. Maybe he would devote more time to the study of human physiology when he came back to school.

If he ever returned.

He mentally shook his head as Professor Hawkins stowed the equipment back into the small black bag. "Please deliver the vials to my home this evening or tomorrow. I will have my colleagues ready to test the fresh samples and see what we can find. I live down in Withersbend, the first yellow house by the flower shop."

"I'll do the best I can to be there."

Professor Hawkins gave him an apologetic glance. "I'm sorry I can't provide a place for you to stay tonight. But by tomorrow I might locate something."

"It's alright. Cass knows the streets of Belhold better than anyone I know."

A slight smile came to the professor's face. "Given what you've shared about her, she is quite the survivor: avoiding the Purges all these years, existing along the dead zone, never caught. It some ways, it makes sense that nature would give a girl like her this immunity. It's as if the universe wants her to survive."

Theo laughed. "Or Elaeros."

Professor Hawkins sat back and folded his hands. "Yes, Elaeros."

The bells began to ring outside. Both men glanced at the window. "My class starts soon," Professor Hawkins said, rising.

"And I should be off before I'm discovered here."

"Be careful, Master Theo." Theo turned to find the professor looking at him with a mixture of emotion in his eyes. "This world needs a person like you. Someone who will search for the truth no matter the cost. You are a much better man than I am."

Theo shook his head. "Not all of us can be visible. If it weren't for you and the others working in the shadows, I wouldn't have had anyone to turn to. We each play our part, and hopefully together we will make this world a better place for everyone."

Professor Hawkins bowed. "Thank you."

"Goodbye, Professor."

"Goodbye, Master Theo. You take with you my best wishes and prayers for your success."

Theo headed out with the black bag tucked under his arm. The rain had stopped, but the dark clouds would hopefully provide covering for him to quietly make his way to the back gate and away from those watching the university. Then once he reached Cass, they could finally start to unravel the secret of her blood.

13

THEO SAT ACROSS FROM CASS THAT AFTERNOON, the glass syringes, tubing, and needles spread out on top of his coat, which he'd draped over the crate between them. The rain had left humidity and sunlight behind. Cass glanced at the door, then back at Theo. A slight shiver went down her back despite the heated air. She could swear the Mist had risen at least a foot during Theo's absence. Was that even possible? Another shiver rippled across her as she turned her attention back to Theo.

"Alright," she said, taking a deep breath as she eyed the needle. The sharp point made her cringe, but at least she could focus on that instead of the Mist. "So you'll prick me with that gadget, take some of my blood, and your professor friends will be able to figure out why the Mist doesn't affect me?"

Theo nodded. "Yes. At least, that's what Professor Hawkins believes."

Cass let out a long, steady breath and placed her hand on the crate, palm up.

Theo hesitated. "I've never done this, so it might take a couple tries." He went around the crate and knelt beside Cass. He picked up the needle and attached the first glass vial.

"I'm curious. Why are you doing this instead of your professor?"

"Everything must be in absolute secrecy. It is better for me to take your blood, then drop it off at his home."

"Why not just meet at his house?"

Theo shook his head as he carefully finished preparing the needle. "We're not sure how many eyes are watching. And I haven't figured out if the Staggs and others are after just me, or if they know about you. The less you're seen, the better."

"How many times am I going to have to do this?" Cass asked.

Theo paused. "I'm not sure. This sample will be enough to start their testing. But they may need more. That is why I must keep you safe and out of view."

Cass made a face. "I feel like a prized chicken."

Theo grinned. "No, you're worth a lot more than a prized chicken."

"Alright," he said a couple seconds later. "Here we go." He wiped the area with a clean cloth and studied the inside of her arm, then brought the needle forward. With careful angling, he inserted the needle. Cass let out a gasp, but kept her arm steady.

Blood appeared. He slowly pulled on the syringe as the red liquid filled the glass. Cass bit her lip. When the blood reached the measured level, Theo pulled the needle back, then popped it off, grabbed one of the glass vials from a nearby wooden box, placed the collected blood inside, and topped it off with a stopper.

He looked over at her. "How are you doing?"

Cass gave him a weak smile. "I'm doing good."

"Ready for another one?"

She nodded without speaking.

He placed the filled vial in the box, readied a new needle and syringe, then proceeded until there were three vials in all.

"Professor Hawkins said this should be enough to get them started," he said as he bandaged her arm.

"I'm glad that's done."

"Me, too." The shadows inside the small area were longer as the sun descended. "I'll head to his house now to hand this over. The fresher the samples, the better."

Cass looked down at her arm. "It's hard to believe that something inside of me could be so important."

Theo lifted the box. "I've heard it said that blood is life. In this case, there is a chance your blood might very well bring life back to this world."

She glanced up. "And if not?"

Theo shook his head. "I don't know."

"Captain Gresley once said that someday Elaeros will make what is broken whole again. Is that true?"

He nodded. "I've read that as well. But I'm not sure what it means exactly, much less when that would be. The world might become even more broken before it is restored. We've already seen the possibility of it worsening."

"That's not a pleasant thought."

"I agree. But I must be off before it gets too late." He headed for the door, the black valise held firmly in one hand.

Cass rubbed her arms, her thoughts returning to the Mist. "Theo?"

He stopped and looked back. "Yes?"

"You'll be coming back tonight, right?"

"Yes, unless something happens."

Her lips twitched. "Do you need to me to tag along behind and watch your back? I know the streets of Belhold well."

"Tempting, but I want you to stay safe."

"I feel the same way about you."

His tense expression melted into a smile. "I'll be back. I promise."

Her face fell. "You shouldn't promise things like that."

"Then I will do my best to make sure I don't break that promise."

Before Cass could say more, Theo was gone.

14

CASS STUDIED THE TINY PRICK ON HER ARM AFTER removing the bandage a short time later. It hadn't hurt, at least not that much. And it had been fascinating—and terrifying—to watch her blood drawn through the syringe, filling the glass container with deep red.

She turned her attention to the sack near the corner where their gliders were hidden. She'd been able to buy potatoes, a handful of apples, and hard biscuits in the district over. They would last for a while and keep hunger at bay. And she'd found an old tattered tunic for Theo. Tomorrow, they would head west. Hopefully the old tenements in the river district would provide a place for them to stay. Then after that—

She plopped down by the crate they were using as a makeshift table. Theo probably wouldn't be back for an hour, and by then it would be evening. She began to tap her fingers across her knees. She wasn't used to sitting in one place for a long period of time. Her street days had been spent always looking for her next meal or a place to hide. And the *Daedalus* had always kept her busy.

The *Daedalus*.

Her fingers paused. Had any of the crew survived? She gripped her kneecap. Of course. They had to have. She'd seen glider pods only once in the bowels of the ship: vehicles used in case of an emergency. Able to glide farther and faster than a human glider, and ready to be launched within minutes.

Her crewmates had to have escaped. At least some. But to where? What area was safe enough along the western mountains?

She peered toward the door. Beautiful blue sky peeked through as if it had been washed by the rain that morning and left radiant. Elaeros. God of the air. With a name like that, no wonder Captain Gresley had believed in him.

Elaeros, she breathed inwardly. *Let them be alive. Keep them safe.*

Theo had sent out inquiries along the most notable docks across the sky before they had fled. Maybe a message had arrived in their absence. *I hope so.*

Conversation interrupted her thoughts.

"Someone said they heard voices coming from somewhere along the first floor," said a man.

"Who?" a second man asked, his voice hoarser.

"One of the girls."

The first man scoffed. "You know they're always telling tales. They also believe in ghosts and think the factory is haunted."

"But still," said the first man, "it's worth investigating."

"I think we should be more worried about the Mist. Is it me or does it seem even closer than yesterday?"

Cass froze. She glanced at the door, then the crates. Where to hide? She couldn't afford to be found. If she was, there was a chance they would search the room and find the gliders.

"Yeah, it does seem closer."

"We should be evacuating instead of searching for some ghost," the hoarse man continued. "What if we wake up tomorrow with the Mist surrounding us?"

A dangerous plan entered her head. Before she could talk herself out of it, Cass jumped to her feet, grabbed the sack of food, and dashed for the door. She was going to take advantage of their ghost story.

"Hey! There goes someone!"

Cass heard the shout as she exited the storage room and ran for the corner of the factory. Ahead the Mist shimmered like the lapping waves of a lake. For one moment her heart stopped, and she couldn't breathe. Was she really going to plunge right into it? The moment passed and she ran.

"What is she doing? She's going into the Mist?"

She heard footsteps behind her. "Wait! Stop! What are you doing?"

Five feet. Three feet.

Cass hurled herself into the Mist and then stumbled down the steep embankment. She lost her balance, fell, and kept sliding. Seconds later, she came to a stop, her backside wet with mud. She glanced over her shoulder, toward the factory. Two men appeared along the edge.

"Did you see that?"

"Yeah, what the gales just happened? She threw herself right into the Mist."

"Is she . . . Turning?"

Cass slowly rose to her feet. This was the most daring part, but she wanted to make sure she wasn't followed. Or that her secret was discovered. She quickly wiped mud across her face, then twisted around and let out a low growl. Slowly she started back up the hill, digging her fingers into the mud, crawling on her knees. Huff, huff. Growl.

"She—she's Turned!"

"Crazy scrounger!"

The two men spun around, one falling in the process.

"Come on!" The guard grabbed his partner. "We gotta get out of here!" He yanked him up, and both fled toward the factory.

Cass stopped near the Mist's edge. She was cold and wet,

but at least the men were gone. And they wouldn't be coming back for her.

She'd never been caught, and she wouldn't start now.

She went back down the hill, grabbed the sack of food she'd dropped, and headed west. She would walk along the Mist's perimeter until she left the Steelhold.

Twenty minutes later, she reached the first set of houses in the next district: dingy, narrow buildings where the families of factory workers lived. At least a fourth of them were submerged in the Mist. Cass swallowed back the bile in her throat as she moved among the empty houses. Between the dying light and the growing shadows, the block looked like a ghost town.

A door swung nearby, causing her to jump. She clutched the bag to her chest and stared at the spot. Just the wind, right?

She crept along the deserted street, watching for any movement, listening for any sound. It was eerily quiet, especially this close to the border. Where were the people? The families? Children? How many had Turned when the Mist took this area?

She shuddered. She didn't want to think about it. At least with a Purge, if people were given enough advance notice, there was a chance to escape. But with how fast the Mist was rising, a person would be caught unaware.

She stopped and looked around at the bare, shabby tenements. There were probably supplies in those flats: food, clothing, maybe even some sterlings.

She still recoiled at the thought of benefiting from lives destroyed by the Mist. But she was a survivor. She took in a deep breath and straightened up. And surviving meant taking what she could. After all, the Turned no longer needed those things.

She crept toward the closest door. It was shut tight. Did that mean no one was inside, or had the occupants Turned and never left? Without her revolver, she'd need to be careful.

She turned the knob and carefully opened the door. No

sound. Slowly she made her way along a hallway. The interior was dark, so she kept a hand on the wall and headed to the back, where she assumed the kitchen was. She found a few potatoes, a small round of cheese, and a handful of eggs. She carefully wrapped the eggs, then placed all the food in her pack.

Checking again and listening, she went back down the hall and up the stairs. A dark-blue skirt, an old overcoat, and a clean blouse. Even better, a basin with old washing water sat on a rickety dresser. She washed the mud from her face, then changed out of her clothes and into the blouse and skirt, which was only a little snug. Her boots and stockings were still muddy, but at least the clothes were dry. She rolled her old clothes up into a bundle, stuffed them in with the food, then headed out. The overcoat looked like it would fit Theo. Perfect. And it didn't cost her a sterling.

Time to leave. It was growing too dark to see. If she desired more supplies, she could come back tomorrow. Right now, she needed to find a place to wait for Theo.

A block later, and after checking for anyone watching, Cass left the Mist. A few lights had been lit in the homes at its border, and she could hear low voices on the other side of the thin walls. Someone hummed a tune in the flat next to her, the same song Theo had been humming the night they were in Voxhollow. More shadows spread as the sun finally descended.

Cass slowly walked along the narrow road, wedged between the grimy buildings, and made plans. Theo would be back soon, and she needed to station herself near the metal walkway so she could intercept him.

Just as night fell across the city, she spotted Theo. Cass scrambled up from where she had been sitting as he stepped onto the metal grating.

"Theo," she whispered loudly.

His head whipped around, and he squinted her direction. "Cass?"

"Yes. We can't go back. Someone must have heard us, and two men came to investigate."

Theo was beside her now. "How did you get away?"

"I've been running away from men like them for years," Cass scoffed. "Not even bluecoats have been able to catch me." She wasn't sure how he would feel about her walking through the Mist, so she left that part out.

"What about the gliders?"

"We'll go back for them when it's time."

"So what do we do now?"

She heard the tightness in his voice. He still wasn't used to this way of life.

Cass readjusted the pack on her shoulder. "I thought we'd follow the Mist and head west. Hopefully we can find a place for the night."

He glanced to his left. "Is it me, or has the Mist risen significantly?"

"It has. Probably almost five feet since last night."

"Five feet! In one night?" He seemed to be calculating something. "The Mist will reach this next set of houses in two days. We've got to warn them, Cass."

She hesitated. "We can, and we should. But I'm not sure where they can go."

"They have to go up."

She looked at him. "Theo, these people aren't wanted higher up in Belhold."

"Doesn't matter. We need to at least give them a chance to escape."

Not ideal. The people here probably already knew the danger, being this close to the Mist and seeing their neighborhood swallowed up. But she'd do it for Theo. "Alright, we'll alert those along this street. Then we find a place for the night."

"Agreed. And Sunday, we'll head up ourselves. We're meeting my sister at the church. Hopefully she'll have news for us."

15

A SENSE OF NOSTALGIA FILLED CASS AS SHE AND Theo made their way along the congested streets of Belhold two mornings later. Omnibuses rolled by, pulled by large steam engines, while small wooden carts moved along the sides of the streets with the vendors declaring their wares. The clothes she and Theo wore blended in with this middle tier of society.

It was almost like that morning a year ago when she had been forced to make her way up the mountain city after a Purge. And just like that time, the homes, gardens, and lifestyle of those who had means, although less than the Families like the Winchesters, amazed her.

White curtains fluttered out of open windows. Chickens clucked from behind houses. Fresh vegetables were displayed now that summer had arrived, bringing with it fresh crops. They passed by one small table which held tiny red radishes, bunched together and tied at the stem, ready for purchase. What would it be like to have a home and a garden, and just . . . live? No fears. No wondering where the next meal would come from, no Mist—

"Latest news from the House of Lords!" a voice called out from the corner. A few people started to gather around the crier—a short man with a brown vest across a white shirt and a slouched cap over his dark-brown hair. "Latest news!

As soon as a small crowd had gathered, he began to give details. Theo and Cass stopped along the outer edge of the crowd to hear what he had to say. Just updates on the economy and something about the south district.

"But what about the Purges?" a tall man in the crowd asked. "I've heard there were two last week in Tyromourne. Why isn't there any news about those?"

"Yeah," said another man. "And the Mist is rising. I've heard it's already reached Potters Street."

"It has?" a woman asked, anxiety pitching her tone. "I hadn't heard that."

More voices murmured, a thin veil of panic lacing through them. Some spoke of those farther down the mountain waking up and finding the Mist at their doorsteps and the evacuations along the north side of Belhold.

"I'm sorry, ladies and gentlemen," said the crier. "I can only relate the news handed to me by the House of Lords.

The crowd began to grumble. "What if the Mist reaches our homes here?" an older plump woman near Cass asked. "Why aren't they doing anything to protect us? We're not scroungers. We should be protected!"

"We're the ones who oversee their factories and provide their food."

"They said they would protect us!"

"It's not like we deserve to be abandoned. We're not like those others."

Cass backed away from the crowd, a twisting, burning feeling in her gut. Her hand reached up to the locket around her neck. She realized these people had no idea what it was like to live near the Mist. To live between life and death. They were afraid for their homes and livelihood now, but where was that concern earlier? This wasn't something new. The Mist had been creeping up the mountain for almost two hundred years, displacing families all the time. Or Purging them.

She spun around in disgust. Part of her wanted the Mist to come and take these people. It wouldn't affect her at all since she was immune. It would serve them right.

Theo's hand gently fell across her shoulder. "Let's go, Cass."

"Yes," she said and started marching in the opposite direction of the crowd.

A minute later, Theo spoke as they crossed a narrow street and started up a terraced hill. "They don't understand what it's like. All those people have ever known is safety and comfort inside the city."

"I know." Her hand clenched around the drawstring of her pack. She let out a long breath. "I know." But would it make a difference if they did? She wasn't sure. After all, the House of Lords knew about the people's plight and still ordered Purges. It wasn't like these people didn't know about the Purges, either. It just hadn't affected them. Same with the Mist.

Until now.

Those thoughts churned inside her head as they climbed the hill. If Theo's friends were successful in finding a way to use her blood, those people would be saved without ever knowing what it had cost. What it'd cost her parents. What it'd cost all those forced into the Mist to make room for others.

Maybe I don't want to help humanity.

Her boots clapped against the cobblestone, and her legs burned as they traversed upward. Perhaps the Mist rising was a punishment for those who had lived along the mountains and let others die for them. Who was she to stop the coming retribution? She felt her anger growing. Then her eye caught Theo's back as he trudged on ahead of her, and the burning inside her heart dimmed, replaced by a tender ache as she studied the man ahead of her, his dark hair glinting in the sunlight, his long, lean body moving forward with purposeful strides, the tattered jacket she had found tight across his shoulders. Theo had also paid a price, and yet he still worked tirelessly toward a cure.

The way she was thinking was no better than that crowd or the House of Lords. Ashamed, Cass hurried to catch up to Theo. She would rather be like him.

As they came over the ridge of homes, the glint of color caught her eye, and a sigh escaped her lips. The beautiful building with colored-glass windows stood across the valley, along the upper part of the next hill, with white-washed walls and a steeple reaching toward the sun. The place where she first laid eyes on Theo.

"What is that building?" she asked as they continued down again along the street, the narrow homes hiding the building from view.

"Building?" Theo asked.

"The one with the beautiful glass windows? The one where we first met."

"You mean the church?"

"Church?" Cass frowned. She'd heard the word before in reference to Elaeros. "Is that where Elaeros lives?"

"Elaeros?" Theo laughed. "No. There is no building that can contain him. He is everywhere." He swept his hand around. "In the very air that we breathe."

"But if he *did* live in a building, I'm sure it would be that one," Cass said. After all, only someone really special could live in such a lovely place. "Wait." She stopped. "Is that where we're going?"

"Yes. Adora said she would meet me near here and let me know everything she discovered from the other night."

Cass glanced down at her outfit. She still wore the blouse and long skirt she had found yesterday. It was clean and nice, but not fancy. Not the sort of thing she had seen the ladies wearing in that remarkable building. "Are we going inside?"

Theo laughed. "No." But there was a hint of disquiet in his eyes as the church came back into view. Cass wondered if he was remembering that day as well, and how she had been treated.

"We'll wait here," he said minutes later. He moved toward the wall next to a home with bright-red flowers in boxes below the windows, folded his arms, and waited.

Cass stood beside him, the church almost hidden from them by a large maple tree growing on the street corner. To the left and two houses down was the small alley where she had first seen Theo. Who would have believed a year later she'd be standing here with the same young man who had gazed at her so curiously?

She leaned back against the wall and felt the sunshine soak in and warm her face. She closed her eyes. The faintest sounds of music drifted along the air, the same tune Theo sometimes hummed. Who was Elaeros really? He seemed to be much more than a distant being worshipped in a house of colored glass.

And what did he think of her?

Bells chimed a minute later, followed by the opening of the double doors. People dressed in suits and bright-colored gowns exited the building, following the steps down to the street and leaving the tinkling of laughter and conversation in the air. The two of them waited for Adora. They didn't have to wait long. She was dressed in a deep burgundy gown and stylish hat with her hair falling in long blond curls behind her.

Theo's Aunt Maude followed, face and attire both dull. How was Adora going to escape the crowd and her aunt to meet them?

Adora reached the bottom of the stairs and looked around. Seconds later, her eyes met theirs. She tugged at her gloves as if adjusting their fit. Cass spotted a small white piece of paper fall. Before anyone could notice, Adora's boot covered the note. She spoke for a few minutes to the young people near her, then scooted her foot toward the wall.

"Smart idea, Adora," Theo whispered.

They waited as the people dispersed, most taking steam-powered buggies home, a few others heading toward a nearby platform where zippers waited. Cass shifted as time ticked by. Finally, the last few stragglers climbed into their vehicle and left, leaving the area in front of the church empty.

Theo lingered a few more minutes. "Stay here," he said and moved away from the tree.

It didn't take him long to find the tiny note. He picked it up, turned it around, and read it. Then he placed it in the pocket of his coat before rejoining Cass. She gave him a quizzical look.

"Where's Adora?" she whispered.

"We're meeting her later at a tea room."

"Tea room?"

"Yes, one in the district over."

"When?"

"Two in the afternoon."

Cass looked down at her outfit again. Good thing she'd found that clean skirt. Hopefully it would be passable for a setting like a tea room. She'd never been to one, but it sounded elegant. She nodded. "Let's go."

16

CHESTER LANE. ONE OF THE MAIN THOROUGHFARES of Belhold, and one that Cass had never visited. Bluecoats were notorious for stopping those who didn't appear to belong. So far, none of the other pedestrians had looked her direction. Which meant she was fitting in fine.

With her arm looped in Theo's, they walked along the cobblestone street. Flower vendors showed their wares: bright-red, brilliant-yellow, and deep-purple flowers of every size and shape. There were hat shops, clothing shops, and even a toy shop with carefully handcrafted wooden toys on display behind wide-paned windows.

The shops reminded her of the ruined cities she scavenged during her dives. The only difference was these ones were bustling with people and life, full shelves, and vibrant conversation.

Two blocks down, she spotted a sign with curved letters: Miss Thompson's Tea Room. Outside were a couple waist-high wooden tables—two people around one and three people around the other. Cups of steaming tea and a plate of small, round biscuits and luscious-looking strawberries sat atop both. Her mouth began to water.

No one glanced their way as Theo held the door and gently

guided Cass inside. Her heart stopped for a moment as her senses took in the room. The heavenly aroma of warm biscuits and the earthy scent of tea filled the air. Sage green papered the walls, and wine-colored curtains accented the windows. Paintings of landscapes, flowers in vases, and varieties of fruit provided pleasing decor. Tables were scattered around the room, most surrounded by customers. Women dressed in dark gowns covered with white, frilly aprons and matching caps brought plates of food and tea to those seated.

A hand rose and waved near the back of the room. Adora leaned over so she could be seen and waved again. A dual feeling of admiration and self-consciousness filled Cass's chest as she and Theo made their way to the back table. Adora was the loveliest woman Cass had ever met. And the smartest, too. Compared to her, Cass felt plain, simple, and ignorant.

"I'm so glad to see the both of you." Adora stood to give Cass a quick hug, then gave her brother a kiss on the cheek. "I've missed you."

"I'm missed you as well, Adora." Theo looked around. "Aunt Maude isn't here, is she?"

"I told her I was meeting some friends, and she claimed to have a headache and went home."

Theo let out his breath. "Good." He looked at his sister. "How did you explain my disappearance?"

Adora retook her seat. "I told her you were suddenly called away on business and were taking Cass back to Belhold. She appeared satisfied by that explanation."

"And Salomon Staggs?"

She smiled. "First, tea."

Even as she said that, one of the serving women came with a silver tray. She placed a steaming teapot, a plate of biscuits, a small bowl of strawberries, and three cups onto the table. "Enjoy," she said with a smile, her eyes lingering on Theo.

"Thank you," Adora said sweetly.

The young woman curtsied and left.

Adora poured the tea and gestured to the biscuits. Cass took one and broke off a piece. It melted in her mouth. Her eyes widened as she savored the taste. She'd never had anything like it.

"Do you like it?"

Cass swallowed hurriedly. "Yes!"

Adora smiled. "Try the tea. They have a wonderful blend here."

Cass took a careful sip. A hint of spices in the dark brew perfectly complemented the biscuit. Is this what it was like to be rich? Such wonderful things to eat and drink?

Theo's biscuit lay untouched, although he did take a sip of the tea. "So," he said, "what happened?"

Adora placed her teacup back on its matching saucer. "I handled Salomon Staggs, just like I told you I would. At first he didn't believe me when I said you were suddenly called away on a trip. So I asked him if he was declaring me a liar." Her eyes danced at Theo. "As you know, I didn't lie. You did go on a trip, but he didn't need to know the details. And he couldn't outright accuse me of lying in front of the bluecoats and that strange man with the metal mask. A gentleman doesn't do such things. I told him that when you returned, I would be happy to convey any message he had for you. Salomon declined my offer. Then he said he couldn't see what his son saw in me." Adora's lips twitched. "I didn't respond. Instead, I most politely saw him out of the manse."

"William is interested in you?" Cass couldn't miss the look of disgust on Theo's face. She wondered who this man was to elicit such a response.

"Trust me, I see nothing of note in William Staggs. His ego is staggering, and he clings to his family name. You do not need to worry about me, brother."

Theo's lips were a thin line. "That's good to know."

Cass suddenly laughed.

Theo glanced over at her and raised an eyebrow.

Cass shook her head. "It's nothing." But she continued to smile as Theo probed Adora for more information. The relationship between brother and sister was new to her, and it brought a spark of joy to her heart just watching them.

"Oh, yes." Adora reached for the small reticule that sat in her lap—an ornate little purse embroidered with daisies and trimmed with lace. She opened it and pulled out a folded piece of paper. "This arrived yesterday. I hope you don't mind, Theo, but I took the liberty of opening it. It's an answer to your inquiries about an airship."

"The *Daedalus*?" Cass nearly upset her tea.

"Yes." Adora glanced at her. "That was your airship, correct?"

"Yes." Cass nodded her head vigorously, her heart beating madly. "Does it say what happened to the crew?"

"Not necessarily. It is from a Bert, and the note was posted from Decadenn."

"Bert." Cass's eyes swelled with tears. He lived. She brought a trembling hand to her mouth. How many others survived? *Thank you* she thought. She pressed her lips shut, afraid that if she talked, she would start crying and wouldn't be able to stop.

Theo reached over and gave her hand a squeeze. "Could I see the note, Adora?" he inquired. "Instead of you just telling me about it?"

Adora blushed slightly as he grinned at her and handed him the small piece of paper. Theo read it, face expressionless. Cass was eager to see it, too, but forced herself to wait.

Theo looked up. "Thank you, Adora."

"Is there anything else I can do, Theo?"

He shook his head and placed the note in his pocket like he had with the other. "Not at this moment."

"What do you plan on doing next?"

Theo looked at Cass, then at Adora. "I think we should head to Decadenn and reunite with whoever is left from the *Daedalus*. The problem is, I only have a handful of sterlings, maybe enough for one second- or third-class ticket."

Adora reached for her reticule again. "I might have enough to provide you with another." She pulled out a couple paperbacks and discreetly handed them to Theo.

"Third class, but it will do."

Adora laughed. "You're experiencing new things every day. Consider this one of them." Then she grew serious. "What about food, lodging, clothing?"

Theo looked at Cass again. "Cass has been showing me how to survive." He smiled at her disarmingly then turned back to Adora, growing serious again. "It's better this way. Less chance of being found."

"You may be right. Salomon Staggs never said why he was looking for you that night. Is it really because you found a cure?"

"Yes, I'm even more sure of it now."

"But you won't tell me what it is."

"I know you wouldn't speak of it to Salomon Staggs or anyone else, but I also wouldn't want you to lie. Just as you have protected me, Adora, let me now protect you. Trust me. When I think it's safe and I have a definite answer, you'll be the first to know." His face softened into a smile. "It truly is a miracle, Adora. Cass herself is a miracle."

Cass shifted uncomfortably at that. She didn't feel like a miracle. She was just Cassiopeia, a young woman who happened to have a rare and strange immunity to the Mist. Strange. Yes, that fit her more.

"You make me want to know even more now, Theo."

Adora sighed at her brother's immobile expression and her eyes drifted past them. "I've heard the Mist is gaining ground every day. I hope you can share your discovery soon. We need a cure now, more than ever. But," she looked at her brother again, "I understand and agree with your decision. If there are those against a cure, you need to stay hidden, although I don't understand why anyone wouldn't want the Mist eradicated."

I agree. Cass took a sip of her tea.

Adora gave her head a shake and looked at them brightly. "Now, finish the rest of these biscuits and strawberries. I doubt you've had a good meal in the last two days. And, Theo, please send me a note once you arrive in Decadenn. I want to know you both arrived safely."

"I will." He finally picked up the biscuit and took a bite. "These are good!"

"Better than Hannah's, but don't tell her that," Adora said with a wink.

Cass took another strawberry. Adora was right. They should eat now and regain their strength so they could head to Decadenn and find the crew from the *Daedalus*.

At least those who survived.

17

THEO AND CASS STOOD ON THE DOCKING DECK before a massive cargo airship. The dirigible was twice the size of the *Daedalus*, with two stacks piping steam into the air, a bloated gasbag, and a metal cargo hold. It was an ugly ship, but it was taking passengers along with its usual load, and so it would do.

A short, stocky man with a dark-blue cap stood at the top of the plank that led into the cargo hold with a wooden board and clip in hand. He glanced over the board at Theo and Cass. "Lookin' for passage?"

"Yes," Theo told him as he led the way up the plank.

"Where to?"

"Decadenn. I was told your ship was heading there."

"Yep." The man narrowed his eyes. "Only have space in the steerage. No rooms, nothing fancy. You sure you're not looking for a passenger ship? Your clothes are nicer than the passage we offer."

"We've fallen on hard times."

The man snorted. "Haven't we all?" He wrote something down on his board. "Escaping the Mist?"

"Something like that."

He placed the board under his arm. "Well, it doesn't matter to me as long as you have the sterlings for the trip. Ten each."

Cass almost gasped out loud. That seemed like a lot just to travel to Decadenn. Theo, however, didn't seem fazed as he pulled out the wad of sterlings, counted out twenty, and handed the bills to the man. She noticed there were only three left as he put the rest back in his pocket. Good thing she'd snagged a few more supplies from those houses in the Mist the other day.

The man stepped back. "On you go."

Theo entered the hold first, followed by Cass. Unlike the *Daedalus*, this ship's deck and hold were attached to the airbag with no external decks. Engines hummed within the large space, currently filled with crates tied down to the floor and metal frame. To her left and up a set of metal stairs, she spotted the front cabin from where the ship was guided. Above them was a crisscross of metal walkways, nets, floors, and more crates, along with a few hammocks that had been hung along the other side of the hold. The air smelled like dust and oil.

"You're not allowed on the second deck, and there are buckets in the back of the ship for privy. Water is held in the barrels to your left. Take only what you need. I hope you brought your own food?" He eyed them.

Cass held up the bag. "We have everything we need."

"Good. Go ahead and make yourselves comfortable. We leave sometime in the next hour. Should take two weeks to get to Decadenn as long as the weather holds out."

The man turned when Theo called out. "I'm sorry. We didn't get your name."

The man glanced back. "George. I'm the first mate. Welcome aboard the *Buxmore*."

They headed toward the back of the ship and found a small area between the crates. Portholes were staggered along the metal wall, allowing some light in, but most of the hold was dark and filled with shadows. Cass swore she heard a rat squeak on the other side of the wooden boxes. But she was used to rats, and a pot for personal use was a luxury compared to other accommodations in her past.

"Hungry?" she asked.

"Yes."

She reached inside for a potato. "Here you go."

After a bite, he grimaced. "Not quite what I'm used to."

"You're probably used to cooked potatoes."

"Well, yes."

Cass took another one for herself and started munching on it like it was an apple. Ages ago, she would actually pretend it was an apple and she was the daughter of a rich merchant who only had time for fancy dresses, ribbons, and sweet, crunchy apples. She smiled to herself. Here she was, sitting with a man who'd actually grown up that way. Minus the fancy dresses and ribbons.

"How much food do we have left?" Theo asked.

"Enough to see us through our voyage to Decadenn if we ration it out."

Cass slid down the side of the crate and drew her legs up underneath the folds of her skirt. She felt the airship shift beneath her as it prepared for departure, and she rested her head on her knees. A feeling of hopelessness suddenly gripped her heart. What if nothing came of using her blood? What if surviving like this—living on potatoes, traveling like vagabonds—caused Theo to leave her? What if there was no future and the Mist consumed everything, leaving her all alone?

A hole opened up inside her chest. She swallowed the lump inside her throat.

She lifted her head and gazed before her. *I've always been a survivor up to now. And if Theo and Captain Gresley are right, even if the Mist takes everyone else, I won't be alone. Not if Elaeros really exists and he is everywhere.* The thought gave her some comfort.

OVER THE FIRST FEW DAYS, THEO SEEMED FINE. HE walked around the hold and studied the ship. Then he grew quiet and sat beside a porthole and watched the clouds drift by. As the second week approached, he kept pacing the steerage like a caged animal.

"Want something to eat?" Cass asked, holding up a hard, crusty biscuit as she sat on a nearby crate. She knew Theo wasn't getting enough to eat. She was already rationing her own portions, but maybe if she went without every other day, she could give him more. She was used to going without.

"No."

"What?"

He turned around. "I know you've been giving me some of your food."

She didn't think he'd been watching her that closely. "I don't need as much as you do."

"But you do need some. I will not take yours."

"But I'm used to it."

He scowled. "That doesn't mean you should give me your portions. I'm not as weak as you think I am."

Her eyes widened, and her pulse sped up. "I don't think you're weak."

"You think since I live on a sky island I can't go through hardship."

Cass jumped down from the crate. "I never said anything like that!"

"But you've thought it!"

They glared at each other.

"Fine." She spun right and headed down the corridor inside the dirigible. She was too angry right now to think clearly. She had just wanted to help him.

She bypassed the rows of crates, moving toward the front of the ship. They weren't supposed to go near the front cabin or the second deck, but right now, she needed space.

Cass came to a porthole just beyond the enclosure where the captain and the crew were working. The rim was wide enough for her to sit next to the window. She hauled herself up and curled like a cat on a windowsill. Her heart still beat with hard, heavy beats, and her whole body was flushed.

The view began to calm her mind and body. It was a clear day, with a blue sky spreading as far as the eye could see, the Mist below billowing, then sinking like the waves on a lake.

She let a few hot tears escape, then pulled her legs in tight and hid her face. She had to admit Theo was right. She had never been quite able to let go of the idea that he was still an echelon and couldn't handle the hardship they were going through right now. And she wasn't giving him a chance.

She felt a small wisp of cool air brush her legs. It felt good. Really good.

Wait.

She brought her head up. She shouldn't be feeling any breeze—

The porthole window began to swing out as the *Buxmore* eased right at a slight angle.

Gales! Cass swung her legs around and moved to jump down, but something held her fast. The pack on her back. She glanced over her shoulder. It was stuck on something.

The window swung out even more as the dirigible entered the turn.

She pulled again and heard a ripping sound. Cold panic shot through her body. No! They couldn't lose the pack. It contained all the food they had left.

Think, Cass, think.

Maybe if she took off the pack, she could figure out what it was stuck on.

Cass slowly pulled the straps down and brought her arms out one at a time, then twisted around while gripping the pack tightly in one hand. There. It was caught on the hook that secured the porthole shut. Whoever had opened this window hadn't secured it properly afterward.

Twisting further around, she brought her legs up and crouched along the rim. There was a gap the size of her hand between the rim and the window. One false move and she would fall out.

She looked over her shoulder. The porthole was too high for her to crawl down and pull the pack free. This was her only choice. She took in a deep breath, then reached for the pack. It was stuck tight. There must have been a small hole or tear at the bottom that caused it to be caught.

She inched closer. *If I just tug it this way—*

A gust of wind caught the window and sent it flying higher with a loud creak. Cass grasped the edge of the rim with her left hand, her fingertips curled around the lip as she swayed toward the hole. She tried to reach for the window with her other hand, but the only gap was near the hinge. The window would crush her fingers once it fell back into place.

Her heart rushed up her throat as the rest of her body went cold. Her vision narrowed until all she could see was her pack and the Mist rolling below. Her fingers grew numb as they gripped the rim.

Save the pack or throw herself to the floor of the ship?

She swallowed. If she died, any chance of using her blood went with her.

Cass swiveled along the rim and lowered her legs. Maybe if the pack remained steadfast, she could pull something over to stand on and free it, if the contents didn't spill out first—

Two hands gripped her waist.

Cass let out a muffled cry and kicked back.

"Ow! Cass, it's just me!"

"Theo?"

"Yes. Let me help you."

"Theo . . ." Cass bit her lip to keep from crying. She let go of the rim, and Theo lowered her to the floor. "The pack! Can you get the pack? It's stuck on the window hook."

Without answering, he reached up and, seconds later, brought the pack down. At the same moment, the window swung open again. "Cass, what in the gales were you thinking?" He sounded more shaken than angry. "You were sitting by an open window?"

Cass took the pack from his hands and thankfully hugged it to herself. "I didn't know it was open until it swung away from me. Then the pack got caught, and I could barely hold on. We almost lost everything!" She shook as the last few terrifying minutes came crashing down on her.

Theo ran his hand through his hair. "I'm just glad I found you, Cass." He added, "I'm sorry for what I said."

Cass bit back a wave of shame. "You didn't say anything wrong. It—it was me. You were right. I didn't believe in you."

"And I assumed things about you." Theo sighed. "We were both wrong."

Seconds ticked by until Theo cleared his throat. "Now let's see where we are. You said we had enough to make it to Decadenn."

Cass nodded. He was right. She did say that. And they did, barely.

Theo continued on. "Listen. I do trust you to take care of the food. And anything else I don't know about, because you're better at this than I am. But I need you to trust that I'm not such an echelon that I can't handle hardship." He met her eyes. "We're in this together."

Cass studied his face. They *were* in this together. Which meant they had to trust each other. It wasn't her place to carry the burden alone. "Yes, we are."

THEY ARRIVED IN DECADENN FIVE DAYS LATER. BY the time the ship docked along one of the walkways, Cass was more than ready to escape the *Buxmore* and smell fresh air again and feel the wind on her face.

Like the previous times she had visited Decadenn, she felt her breath catch in her throat at the sight of the floating city. The mid-morning sun's rays illuminated the metal buildings in a dazzling display of brilliance and light. The steamshuttle chugged by on a rail set high above the streets. Despite the altitude of the city, the warmth of early summer spread across Decadenn.

Once they were on the metal walkway, Theo stopped and took the familiar piece of paper out of his jacket. "It says here that Bert is currently at dock A. And this is . . ." he peered down the walkway toward a large white sign with a letter on it. "Looks like we are at D. So we have a walk ahead of us."

Cass's heart beat a little faster as they headed toward the street that circled the city of Decadenn and connected the docks that surrounded the perimeter. They knew that Bert had survived because of Theo's note. But what about everyone else? What had happened that day?

"So is the plan the same?" Cass asked. They had talked about what they would do when they first arrived.

"Yes. Meet up with the crew from the *Daedalus* first and find out what happened. I also feel responsible for the loss of the ship, so I'm going to see what I can do to repay them."

Cass nodded. Theo had been insistent about that.

"Then I plan on visiting the Atwoods."

"The Atwoods? You mean one of the Five Families?"

"Yes. If a cure is found in your blood, then we are going to need allies. One of the other Families would be best. I can't fight the Staggs and the others alone."

Cass slowed her steps. "Do you think it'll come down to that?"

"They've already tried killing us once. I don't think they'll stop trying. And we don't know if Salomon has convinced the other houses to follow his lead."

"But what about the Atwoods?"

"Charity has already proven to care about people. She also gave me that warning about the Staggs that night. And her father, though timid, did speak up at the last meeting. It's at least worth talking to them."

Fight the great Families? Cass rubbed her arms despite the warm air. Not only were they racing against time before the Mist covered everything, Luron and the Staggs could be hunting them right now.

Cass glanced around the docks. Crates and barrels lined the wooden walkway that ran the perimeter of the city. Past the walkway, streets entered Decadenn with stores and flats lining both sides. Smoke and steam filled the air.

Although they had been careful, who knew where hidden

informants were, ready to provide information for a couple sterlings. Even now someone could be watching them. She shifted her eyes to the left, where the Mist swirled beyond the railing. In some ways, the Mist was the only safe place for her. No one could follow her there, not without risk. Except for Luron.

Cass shivered. Would it come to that?

They passed Dock C and Dock B. Both were busy, with four ships at each and dozens of workers using cranes or manual labor to unload the ships, stacking barrels of provisions recently arrived from the smaller mountaintop cities dedicated to providing food, materials, and other supplies to the rest of the world. A small stack of crated chickens squawked as they walked by. Next to it sat fifty-pound sacks of potatoes.

"Busy today," Theo murmured.

Cass nodded. Which also meant many eyes in many places.

As the sign for Dock A came into view, Cass scanned the area. There was even more activity here, with five airships ranging from small, nimble merchant ships to large, bulky carriers like the *Buxmore*. There was even a zeppelin for passengers. The dock was crowded, with people pressing against each other from one railing to the other.

Cass grabbed the back of Theo's coat, afraid she would be swept away in the crowd. All she could see were people. At least he was tall enough to see over all these heads. While they moved toward the dock, the rest of the crowd headed for the city. Minutes later, the area cleared, leaving only the workers and hundreds of boxes set up like a maze. As they moved, a voice stood out from the din of workers' conversations.

She let out a breath and released the back of Theo's coat.

". . . place it next to the barrels labeled Brennet."

Her heart stopped. Bert.

She had to know for sure. "Theo! This way." She grabbed his hand and headed to the wall of crates. At the right was a gap. They squeezed between the cartons. A man stood ten feet away, his back to them, holding a board with papers attached. His blond hair was pulled back at the nape of his neck, where a tattoo of a snake wove up into his hairline. She would know that hair and tattoo anywhere.

"Bert!" she yelled and dashed across the wooden planks.

Bert swerved around. "Cass?" His eyes widened, and he lowered the board and papers. "It can't be . . ."

Cass laughed as she halted in front of him. "Yes." She beamed up at his face. "It's me."

18

"CASS," BERT SAID AGAIN, SHOCK FADING INTO A smile, which took over his face. He ran a hand over the top of her head, ruffling her curls. "It really is you."

"What's happening?" Jeremiah came running around a stack of crates, skidded to a stop, and spotted her. "Cass!" he yelled as he caught her up in a big hug. He swung her around. "Cass, I can't believe it's you! Where did you come from? How did you survive?"

Cass couldn't seem to stop laughing. "Jeremiah, you scallywag! Put me down."

Three other men stepped into view. Will, wearing overalls and a bit of grease on his cheek, carrying a wrench in his hand. Cyrus, the most recent diver on the *Daedalus*. And Nate, one of the deck hands.

Briefly she wondered where everyone else was. Had some of them died? Or had they scattered after the *Daedalus* went down?

The others gathered around and everyone started asking questions. Joy bubbled up inside her. She'd missed them. Her family.

"Hold on, hold on." Bert placed his hands up in the air. "Calm down and let Cass speak."

"Yeah, he's right," Will said and gestured Cass toward the middle of her old crewmates.

"So, Cass," Bert asked for everyone. "How in the gales did you survive Voxhollow?"

Cass looked around, spotting Theo beyond the group. She waved him over. "Theo rescued me."

The men swiveled to Theo. He gave them a brief nod. Cass's happiness faltered a little. They obviously held Theo responsible. She would have to convince them Theo was genuinely trustworthy.

"After Bert left with Cyrus, we searched for Theo's family home. And we found it."

Bert's eyes darted between them. "You found the house?"

"Yes. And we found what Theo was looking for."

"Was it worth it?" Bert asked, his tone darkening.

Theo straightened up. "What we discovered down there was extremely important."

Cass wondered if he was going to say more, but he looked at her and gave his head a single shake. Alright, she'd just continue on. "We were discovered by the Turned and had to make a run for it. At the same time, it started raining, so we found another abandoned home. We stayed there for the night and hoped we would be able to rendezvous with all of you the next morning. When day broke, we headed for the nearest hill to start our climb, but then someone showed up."

They were all listening intently.

"Who?" Bert and Will asked at the same time.

"A man with a golden mask. His name is Luron. He was hunting us."

Bert looked at the others and nodded. "We were wondering about him. Spotted him on the patrol ship before the dive into Voxhollow. Go on, Cass."

"Anyway, I had gotten really sick, so I don't remember much

more, other than Theo handing me the box he had retrieved and telling me to run. I did, but then . . ." she broke off as unexpected tears came to her eyes. The rest was just hazy, heat-filled memories, but the terror still gripped her.

Theo stepped up. "When I found her, she was surrounded by Turned. I managed to fight them off and get her up the hill. She was unconscious, but I was able to attach her to my glider and ascend. The hope was to get to the *Daedalus* as fast as possible, to get help for Cass. It was a shock to draw near and find it on fire. At that very moment, flames reached the gasbag and the ship exploded. There was nothing left to do but glide all the way to Duskward and find help there."

"You glided all the way to Duskward?" Jeremiah's voice was filled with awe. "With Cass?"

"Yes. Cass had a high fever and, even when conscious, wasn't coherent enough to glide herself."

Jeremiah let out a long whistle. "That's amazing."

Will leaned in. "Then what happened?"

"An aeroship was making a delivery to Duskward, and I was able to get passage for us back to Belhold. She recovered at my home."

"So what are you doing here?" Bert wanted to know. "And what about the gold-masked guy?"

"He's back, and I believe he's after us again. We've been on the run for a couple weeks now."

"But somehow you got my message."

"Yes, my sister gave me it to me. That's why we're here."

Bert studied Theo for a moment. "So why is this man hunting you?"

Cass and Theo exchanged glances. Cass wanted to tell Bert and the others. They could be allies. But the more people who knew meant more people who could accidently spill something without meaning to. And then even more people could get hurt.

"First, we'd really like to know what happened to the *Daedalus,*" Theo answered.

"Yes, Bert," Cass interjected. Losing it was heartbreaking. She swallowed. "You have no idea how relieved we were to get your note."

Darkness flashed across Bert's gaze again before he spoke. "The patrol ship came back. They demanded to board and said they were searching for something. I asked for their written orders, but they claimed they had verbal orders from the Five Families to stop any ship from entering the area. I pointed out we had already produced papers allowing us passage, and that those papers had been accepted days before. But, without warning, they shot at our ship."

"Scumbags," Jeremiah muttered under his breath. Cyrus said something stronger.

"They hit the bow, and the *Daedalus* caught fire," Bert continued, face grim. "They fired a couple more times, then retreated. We fought the blaze for as long as we could, but whatever substance they used made it impossible to extinguish. I had no choice but to order an evacuation before the flames reached the gasbag. Lives mattered more than the *Daedalus.* Everyone made it to the gliders, and we took off for Tyromourne."

"So everyone survived?" Cass asked, hopefully.

Hurt shadowed his eyes. "No, Patterson and two others went down shortly after we took off."

"Oh." She swallowed against her swelling throat. There had been a gruff kindness to Patterson. He had taken her under his wing when she came on board the *Daedalus.* The loss of him and the others left a hole in her chest.

Bert glared at Theo. "So I'd really like to know why we were shot down and who this masked man is. I think we've earned some answers."

Theo glanced at Cass, then regarded Bert for a moment.

"What I'm about to say cannot leave this group. If this information is leaked, it could cost Cass her life and the lives of entire communities."

There were a couple gasps. Will's eyebrows rose, but Bert narrowed his eyes. "Those are some pretty strong claims."

Theo's jaw tightened. "Yes, they are. That's why I want your word before I say anything else."

Bert looked around at the others. They nodded at him. "You have our word. Especially if talking would endanger Cass."

Theo turned to her. "Would you like to tell them, or would you like me to?"

It dawned on Cass that they would trust it more coming from her. Her heart pounded in her chest at the thought of now sharing the secret she and Theo carried. "I will," she said, her voice cracking.

Theo nodded. "Then let's move to a quieter spot."

"Over there." Bert pointed to an area at the edge of the dock with crates stacked along two sides. An old dirigible floated a few feet away. "The ship is empty, and we're the only ones working this dock, so even if someone walks along the nearby pier, they won't hear us."

Everyone agreed and moved. Once there, Cass straightened, took a breath, and looked at her former crewmembers. No, family. The word brought a measure of calmness, which made it easier to speak. "When Theo originally hired us, it was to find a family heirloom. What we didn't know was it held the cure for the Mist."

"What the—?" Jeremiah sputtered. "A *cure*?"

"Yes. And as Theo told you, we found it."

Exclamations came from the crew. Jeremiah raised his voice. "So you have a cure for the Mist?"

"Sort of. However, the box was lost during our escape from Luron, the masked hunter."

Cyrus swore. "So what good was that trip then? We lost everything!"

"No." Cass looked around at them slowly. "We still have the cure. It's . . . me."

Complete silence.

"You?" Bert eyed her doubtfully.

"Theo left a part of the story out. When he found me, apparently I didn't have my mask fully on. It had been ripped away by the Turned. I don't really remember, because I was sick. When Theo realized I wasn't Turning, he chose to save me instead of reclaiming the box." Cass held out her hands. "There seems to be something inside of me that allows me to breathe the Mist and not Turn. It's the same thing the papers in the box had information about."

"You breathed in the Mist and didn't Turn? You know this for sure?" Bert stared at her with an unreadable look.

"Yes, because I tested it myself. Twice. I can walk, breathe, and probably even live in the Mist and not Turn. Theo believes it's my blood. He's already taken a sample of it to his science friends who are seeing if there is a way they can replicate it. If so, it would benefit everyone."

"You don't Turn?" Jeremiah repeated, seeming dumbstruck. Will had a similar expression on his face.

Cass laughed awkwardly and gave a little shrug. "I guess not."

"That's . . . unbelievable." A ghost of a smile appeared on Bert's face. "And you"— he turned to Theo, now more curious than confrontational—"think that this can be shared with everyone?"

"An ancestor of mine believed so. His research is what we found. And Cass is living proof that it is possible to be immune to the Mist spores. We just need to unlock the secret of her blood."

Jeremiah grinned. "Then we wouldn't need to live in the sky anymore. I could visit the ground, just like a diver."

Just like a diver. Cass's shoulders sagged somewhat. A world where people could move in the Mist would no longer need divers. She shook herself. It meant people could live.

Theo nodded. "The Mist could be studied more closely, and people would be free to move back into the valleys. With more time and without the fear of Turning, there might be a way to eradicate the Mist permanently."

"A world without the Mist," Will murmured, his wrench dangling at his side.

"Yes." Cass's insides squeezed tightly together. Why was she suddenly selfishly focused on having to find another way to make a living? She should be happy that there was a chance everyone could live in the Mist.

Bert folded his arms. "So why hasn't all this been pursued before? Is Cass's blood so rare that she is the only one? You mentioned you had an ancestor that knew there was a solution to the Mist. So why has nothing ever been done with that knowledge?"

The men all turned to Theo, skepticism and wariness in their eyes once more.

Theo looked at them in turn. "I've been asking that almost all of my life, and only recently found anything. It turns out the Five Families have known about this."

"They knew there was a cure for the Mist?" Bert snapped.

"Yes. Or at least that it was out there."

"What the—then why didn't they do anything?" Jeremiah spurted.

"Because of power. The Mist is how they've retained their power. They choose who lives and dies, allocate funds toward the projects they want to see accomplished, and live how they want to. If the Mist disappeared, people would have more freedom, and the Families would lose control."

"Well, that's a load of dung," Jeremiah stated. The others voiced their agreement.

Bert was regarding Theo with suspicion. "How do you know this?"

"Because I'm part of the Five Families."

The men stiffened.

"My real name is Theodore Byron Winchester. I am the head of the Winchester family."

"You're a Winchester?" Jeremiah looked stunned.

"Yes. My grandfather was Crispin Winchester, head of the Alchemy Society."

Bert stabbed a finger at Theo. "So you lied to us."

Theo met Bert's glare. "I chose not to share my full name. I wanted to be able to move without detection or without the bias that comes with the name. I've studied the Mist for years, like my father before me. My main goal has been to find a way to eradicate it. At my grandfather's recent passing, he revealed we had a cure all this time, but it was not in our possession. I've been doing what I could to find it. This isn't for myself or for my family. If it takes risking my life and name, so be it."

Cass came between Theo and Bert and faced the latter. "Bert, I've known Theo's real name for a while now, and I can vouch for him. He wanted to be treated like an ordinary man when he came on board the *Daedalus*. His parents were also hunted down and killed searching for the missing cure. You've got to understand he's had to be careful."

"It's true," Theo said. "The *accident* that took my parents was no accident. Those who want to maintain power will do whatever they can to keep others from finding anything that might change the Mist. Burn a ship"—he shot a glance at Bert— "or take lives."

There was a silence, and then Bert spoke. "I may not believe you at the moment, but I do believe Cass. And if Cass trusts you, then so do I." The others looked at one another and murmured their agreement. Cass's heart warmed. She gave Bert a deep look of thanks. His demeanor softened a little. "So what do we need to do to help?

Cass could almost feel Theo relax. He responded immediately, "The next plan is to meet with the Atwood family."

"Atwoods. Aren't they part of the Five Families?" Cyrus asked.

"Yes. I'm looking for allies."

At the crew's questioning looks, Theo explained. "If there is a way to replicate Cass's immunity, we will need a way to produce and distribute it. I won't be able to do it alone. I have reason to believe the Atwoods would work with us. It was the Atwoods who gave us the necessary paperwork to bypass the patrol and reach Voxhollow. During the House Meetings, the Atwoods seemed predisposed to our cause. I believe I can trust them."

"And what about us?" Bert inquired. "We can't do much. We have no ship and are deeply indebted to Captain Gresley's brother."

Theo nodded. "I can answer that, but first," he looked around at the crew, "I feel the responsibility lies on me. What was still owed on the ship?"

Bert named the sum left on the *Daedalus,* and Theo didn't even blink.

"I have enough to cover that. Where can I meet this Eli so I can clear your debt?"

Bert's eyes slightly widened. "He lives here in Decadenn, down on Grime Row."

"I've been there before," Cass told Theo. "I can go with you."

"Good, then I'll do that. Also, I think having our own ship would be helpful. I confess I'm not very knowledgeable in the area of obtaining one."

Bert looked at him, incredulity in his eyes. "Are you saying you want to buy a ship?"

"Yes," Theo said firmly. "And I would like you to be the crew."

Jeremiah had been listening with his mouth agape. "Just how much money do you have?" he blurted.

Theo grinned. "Enough. And it's about time it was used to

help others rather than just the elite."

"Then why did you hire us all those months ago instead of buying your own ship?" Bert's voice had lost its edge and was now layered with genuine curiosity.

"At the time, I just needed divers and passage. I saw no reason to invest in a full ship. But now, I think having our own transportation and gear would be best. And," he looked at the man before him, "it's a way to make up for the destruction of the *Daedalus*. Consider me the investor in your new enterprise."

"Gales," Jeremiah uttered as the crew broke into excitement.

A slow grin came to Bert's features as he watched the men. He faced Theo. "I might know of a ship. She's smaller than the *Daedalus*, but in good condition and faster, too."

"Excellent," Theo said. "See if you can procure it for us. Let's meet back here in two days. Same time."

Bert stuck out his hand. "Sounds good. Let's shake on it. As we say on the *Daedalus*, our hand is our bond."

Theo took it and they shook vigorously. "I'm glad we were able to find all of you."

Bert nodded. "I am as well. We thought the worst had happened to you, especially Cass. I don't really believe in Elaeros, but I was praying. To see you both survived, it's like a miracle."

Cass stood back, watching, and smiled at the warm feeling still bubbling up inside of her. She was reunited with her family.

19

CASS CAST ONE LAST LOOK BACK AT DOCK A, where the *Daedalus* crew finished up their work carrying crates off the dirigible, before walking away. They had eaten the last of their food that morning. She wasn't sure how they would obtain more or where they might stay the night. And she didn't feel comfortable meeting the Atwood family in her present condition. She smelled terrible, and her hair was matted with filthy curls.

She and Theo headed up a set of stairs to a platform, where people gathered to ride the steamshuttle. Wisps of white cloud drifted overhead. She felt light-headed. Should she ask Theo for a sterling to buy food?

Her cheeks flushed at the thought of asking for money. She had never done such a thing in her life. No, she wouldn't do it.

The steamshuttle came rattling in with a loud huff along the narrow rails, puffing hot white steam into the air as it braked to a stop. At least a dozen people stood on the platform, ready to embark once the shuttle emptied its current occupants.

The doors cranked open, and a stream of people exited the metal tube. A minute later, those gathered began to push inside the shuttle. Cass barely kept pace with Theo and found herself smashed up against the glass as the doors shut. There was a rumble as the shuttle prepared to leave.

Then something caught her eye. There, below the platform, looking up at them. The glint of a gold mask. Then it was gone.

Thoughts of hunger and discomfort fled as Cass craned her head to catch sight of it again as the shuttle pulled from the station. Nothing.

Her breath fogged the window. The air inside was hot and stifling, but she felt cold. It had only been for an instant, but she was sure of what she had seen. Somehow, someway, they were being followed by the very one who had tried to kill them in Voxhollow.

Luron.

Cass turned around to tell Theo but didn't see him. "Theo?" She tried to peer past the people around her, but she could only see torsos and limbs. Her heart beat faster. "Theo?" she said louder.

A hand snaked through the crowd and gripped her sleeve and tugged. Theo. She grasped his fingers, and her heart calmed somewhat, but she still couldn't shake what she had seen outside the window.

The shuttle swayed and rumbled as it made its way through Decadenn, above the streets and through the tall buildings of metal and brick. Cass shivered again. How had Luron found them? Had he been tracking them the entire time?

What do we do? Was anywhere safe?

The shuttle slowed to a stop, and the doors rolled open a minute later. Half of the occupants disembarked. Theo stepped next to Cass as the shuttle filled again. "Sorry. I didn't realize we had separated in the crowd."

She didn't reply as another mob of people pressed inward. The shuttle started again. She glanced up at Theo, but he seemed preoccupied, his eyes staring far off past the window.

Cass watched him. His chin and jaw had a bit of dark stubble, giving him a more rugged look. His hair could use a washing, but it still looked good as it hung in waves along his shoulders.

Her cheeks grew flushed. She had never seen Theo like this. Why was it doing strange things to her? She quickly turned back around, but could now feel the heat between their bodies. That made her flush even more.

Get a hold of yourself.

Minutes later, the shuttle slowed again.

"This is our stop," Theo said and moved toward the door.

Cass stayed close by him as they flowed out of the shuttle with a mob of travelers. Down the wooden steps they went and onto the street. Unlike the industrial side of Decadenn, this section was filled with brick, three-story flats with white shutters and flowerboxes. Narrow arched windows lined the buildings, and the occasional tree had been planted, each one surrounded by a black metal fence.

It reminded her of the neighborhood around the church in Belhold, only denser. Pretty little red flowers bloomed in the boxes. She was surprised flowers had been planted and not some more practical plant, like tomatoes or strawberries. Maybe vegetables struggled in this atmosphere.

Then she remembered Luron.

"Theo." She stopped him as they headed along the cobblestone street.

"Yes?"

She looked over her shoulder, then back at Theo. "I think I saw Luron back at the station."

He stared at her. "What?"

"When we were pulling away from the station near the docks, I'm pretty sure I saw a golden mask. At least, it was golden and it covered a man's face. I don't think that's a popular fashion," she added wryly.

Theo glanced around, like Cass had a moment ago. "This is not good," he muttered. He took her arm and walked faster, striding up the street.

Cass stumbled and caught herself. "Hold on! I can't keep up."

"I'm sorry, but we have to get to the Atwoods as soon as possible."

"But what about Luron?"

His mouth was a straight line. "That's one of the reasons we need to hurry."

THEY STOPPED TWENTY MINUTES LATER IN FRONT of a wrought iron fence that encircled a large brick house. It was twice the size of the homes around it, and two huge trees graced the front yard just beyond the fence. To the left a tower rose from the side of the house, and a wide porch surrounded the first floor. The name was etched on a golden plate that hung to the right side of the gate: Atwood.

Theo pressed on a small dial just below the plaque. Far off, Cass could hear a bell ring. Some seconds later, the double doors opened, and a dapper older gentleman emerged. He was dressed in a dark suit with his grey-streaked hair slicked back and wore white gloves. He reached the gate. "May I ask who is calling at the Atwood residence?"

"Theodore Winchester and guest."

The butler bowed his head. "You are welcome here, sir." He unlatched the gate and swung it wide open.

"Thank you." Theo walked in with Cass close by. The

butler closed the gate and led the way to the porch ahead. At the top of the staircase, the butler stopped near the front door. "Which Atwood do you wish to see today?" he inquired.

"Miss Charity. And her father, if he is available."

"Master Reynard is currently away. But Miss Charity is here. I will let her know she has a guest."

"Thank you . . ."

"Edgar, sir."

"Thank you, Edgar."

He opened the front door and bowed as Theo and Cass entered the home. It was as beautiful inside as it was outside. Wooden floors glistened beneath the chandelier that lit the foyer. Ahead, a grand staircase led to the second floor. Wood panels and ivory wallpaper lined the walls, and beyond the staircase, rich-colored runners lined the floor. The butler led them to the room on the right.

More elegance met Cass's gaze. A light-green settee and two chairs sat before a fireplace. A desk stood in the corner with paper, quill, and ink ready for correspondence. Light spilled in from the windows on one side of the room with a view of a small colorful garden.

Cass sat down quietly in one of the chairs, overwhelmed by the opulence. Theo also took a chair. He looked like he belonged. He looked aristocratic, while she . . .

Once again she was struck by how distant their lives were. They lived in two different worlds. She glanced at her fingers. Short, stubby appendages with her nails chewed to the quick and calluses along her palms from working as a diver. Definitely not a lady's hands.

"It would seem I'm not the only one occupied by my thoughts," Theo remarked lightly.

Cass glanced up. "I guess not."

"Is everything alright?"

"Yes." Cass clasped her hands across her lap.

The door to the sitting room opened, and Edgar the butler walked inside, followed by a stately young woman. "Miss Atwood is here to see you both."

20

CHARITY ATWOOD STOOD FOR A MOMENT INSIDE the doorway next to Edgar. So this was the daughter of one of the Five Families. She was beautiful, like Adora, with an elegant cream-colored gown and matching gloves that contrasted with her rich, dark skin. Her black hair was pulled into two loose rolls that swept around her head. Pearl earrings dangled from her earlobes. She smiled at Cass, revealing lovely, perfect teeth.

Cass felt a wistful twinge in her middle, and she looked away. Charity's smile was just like Captain Gresley's. Big, warm, and beautiful.

"Theo, it is so good to see you." Charity entered the room, and Edgar closed the door quietly after he exited. Theo stood to his feet, and Cass figured she should stand as well. Charity approached the two of them with the same grace that Cass would expect from someone of her status. "And I see you brought a lady friend." She turned her bright smile on Cass.

"Charity, this is Cass."

"Cass . . ."

"Just Cass," Cass said quickly.

"She was one of the divers on the *Daedalus*. The ship you helped me procure papers for to enter Voxhollow."

Her eyebrows rose. "I see. Nice to meet you, Cass." Charity held out her gloved hand and for a moment Cass wasn't sure if she should take it. Her own hands were quite dirty. But Charity didn't seem to care, so Cass took the woman's dainty hand and shook it.

"Nice to meet you, Miss Atwood."

Charity's laugh sounded like bells. "I must say meeting a woman diver is quite a pleasure. I would want to hear about all of your adventures, but I have a feeling this is not a social call." She glanced over at Theo. "Am I correct?"

"Yes."

Her smiled faded a little. "I'm glad to see you here. I hope that means my warning helped you, even just a little." She headed for the settee and sat down. The other two followed suit. "If you can, tell me what happened. But first," she held up her hand, "I'll have a tray brought in. And tea." She rang a tiny porcelain bell from the table nearby.

Seconds later, a maid appeared, dressed in black with a white apron and frilly cap.

"Mary, would you be so kind as to bring the afternoon tea to this room. Servings for three. After that, please see to the guest rooms."

Mary curtsied. "Yes, my lady." She disappeared.

As they waited, Cass listened as Theo once again shared their adventure—from Voxhollow to escaping the manse the night Staggs arrived with a handful of bluecoats. Her attention ebbed and flowed throughout the conversation, caught by the muffled ticking of a clock out in the hallway.

Theo finished, and Charity took in a deep breath. "I had a feeling there was a divide amongst the Five Families concerning the Mist. And I have appreciated how you speak up at the business meetings."

"I think Titus is growing tired of me," Theo remarked.

"Yes, I think he is," Charity agreed with a slight smile. Her face grew earnest. "But tell me, have you made any headway? Did you find anything in Voxhollow?"

Theo exchanged a look with Cass. "Yes," he said slowly.

Just then, Mary arrived with a silver platter. "Your tea, my lady." She crossed the room and placed the platter on a table between the settee and chairs. On top was a plate of small cucumber-and-tomato sandwiches as well as a pot of tea and matching teacups.

Cass breathed in the smells and felt light-headed. That potato this morning had barely filled her stomach. Tomatoes! Her mouth began to water.

Cass tried not to show her eagerness when Charity invited them to partake as she poured the tea. It was so hard to hold back as she bit into the sandwich. The tomato was sweet and tasted like heaven.

"The tomatoes are from my garden," Charity said.

"They're delicious!" Cass exclaimed after a bite.

Charity beamed as she passed out teacups filled with amber liquid. "Enjoy."

"It's amazing what food can do for the body," Theo said with a smile at Charity. He leaned forward. "You asked if I've made any headway into finding information about the Mist. I did. Both in Voxhollow and in my travels since. And that is why I'm here. I need help. But I also want you to be aware that once—once you have the same information we do—you will most likely be in danger. If nothing else, Staggs and the others might come after you for it."

"Is the information worth it?"

Theo looked at her directly. "It could save the world."

She firmly placed her teacup down. "Then I want to help."

"Are you sure?"

"Yes. It is high time the Families did something more than

maintain our own existence. We should be out there, helping people survive. Whatever you've found, whatever cure or information, I want to be a part of it. No matter what."

Theo nodded. "Thank you, Charity." He sat back. "I don't know how much the other Families know about what happened in Voxhollow. As I said, Luron was there, no doubt sent to stop any discovery of the papers left by my ancestors. What I don't know is if Luron discerned another truth that day."

Cass pushed her plate away as she squirmed inside.

Charity sat straight. "Another truth?"

"Luron isn't the only one immune to the Mist."

Charity gasped.

"Cass is also immune."

Charity turned to her, eyes wide.

Cass nodded, feeling awkward as Theo explained. "Her facemask was ripped away during an altercation in the Mist. She never Turned, despite being exposed to the spores for minutes. We also tested her immunity again after arriving back in Belhold."

Cass didn't bother to mention her escapade into the Mist while running from those men at the factory. But now she had actually been exposed three times—and never Turned.

"Cass doesn't Turn?" Charity's wondering eyes gazed at Cass who squirmed again inside. She had already lived much of her life as an oddity: street rat, woman diver, and now a survivor of the Mist.

"No. And her blood might be the cure we've been looking for."

"How?"

"The papers left behind tell of a tiny population of people who were immune to the Bioformin used during the Plague Wars and indicated they would be the key should anything go wrong. There was even a vial of blood with the papers. I took a sample of Cass's blood to one of my professors at Browning and discovered there has been a secret group working toward an answer all this time. My parents were part of this group."

"Did your grandfather know?"

"No. He said nothing until just before he died, but he did seem to suspect their deaths were not accidental."

Charity shook her head. "All this time, there's been help available. Worse, the Five Families have refused to test Luron for a cure, even though they obviously know of his unusual condition."

"We're not certain there is an absolute cure, at least not yet. I'm still waiting to hear back from my professor on whether or not they found the reason why Cass seems to be immune and if that can be used to help the rest of us in any way."

Charity glanced at the window. "We will need that immunity soon with the way the Mist is rising. I've heard that a fourth of Tyromourne has disappeared."

"A fourth?" Cass felt the same shock that appeared on Theo's face. He rose to his feet. "Professor Hawkins doesn't know where I am. I should send word to him by courier."

"But what if Luron sees you?" Cass asked, speaking up for the first time

Charity started. "Luron is here?"

"Yes, at least we think so. Cass believes she saw him while we were on the steamshuttle."

"Then we need to send someone else to the general post in your stead," Charity said. "What about my butler, Edgar?"

Theo gave a quick nod. "Good idea. Have the response sent here."

"But what about Luron?" Cass repeated.

Theo's face grew tense. "That is a possibility. If he saw us on the steamshuttle, he might have suspected I was coming to your home. That means we can't stay here long."

"But where will you go?" Charity asked.

Theo looked at Cass. "I'm not sure yet."

Cass's mind was whirring. "We need to wait for an answer from Professor Hawkins. Here, if this is where the answer will come. Since we're meeting up with the *Daedalus* crew in two days, we will have a ship by then if they were successful. We should be alert if Luron shows up. He might come, but he also might just be watching the place and reporting back. I don't think he'd just walk up to the door and knock. He would bring bluecoats with him at the very least to make his appearance appear legitimate."

"You're right, Cass." Theo gave her a nod and turned. "Charity, I hate to intrude, but would you mind if we stayed here at least one night while we wait for the message?"

"I've already said you can stay both nights. Stay as long as you need until you meet up with this crew of yours."

"It might put you in danger if Luron comes with bluecoats."

Charity lifted her chin. "I would like to see him do that. My family is closely connected with the bluecoats here in Decadenn. Captain Wyndham has long been a friend of my father's. He would send a message or come in person if it came to that. In the meantime, why don't you both freshen up while the guest rooms are being prepared?"

Cass could feel all the grime and sweat from the last few days. "Oh, gales, yes!"

Charity laughed.

"IS THERE SOMETHING BETWEEN YOU TWO?" Charity had returned to her seat in the parlor after showing Cass where to wash and tidy herself.

"What do you mean?" Theo asked.

She gave him a quick smile. "I'm just curious. Watching both of you in the sitting room, it was like you were a team. And you defer to her with respect, even though she is not from the same class."

Theo spoke thoughtfully. "For the last few months all I've done is study, fly on an airship, and run from the Staggs." He let out a little snort. "But I have to admit when I met Cass . . ." He remembered her from that day, with her hair pulled back and a pair of goggles over her eyes, dressed in overalls and carrying a tool.

"She's different," Charity offered.

"Yes." He was surprised how serious he was. "She is candid in her speech and action. In fact, when we first met, she called me an echelon." Charity gave him a puzzled look. Clearly she hadn't spent much time with the lower classes. He coughed. "It's a, er, derogatory term used to describe those who are rich and live on sky islands."

Charity's eyebrows rose. "Oh. And you didn't find that offensive?"

He shrugged. "She was right. I was an echelon. But I've come a long way. And so has Cass. She's curious, not afraid to learn, and one of the more courageous people I've ever met."

"One would have to be courageous to be a diver," Charity agreed.

"Yes." Theo smiled. "She's the one who taught me how to dive. And in return, I started teaching her how to read."

"Read?"

"And more. Use a microscope, study slides."

Charity brushed her skirt. "I can see why you two get along. But Theo, what happens when this is all over?" She looked up at him. "Let's say Cass's blood has the answer and the Mist is constrained or eliminated, what then? Though you are alike, you both come from very different worlds. And the Winchester family will be as much needed in the new world as it is in the old, especially as the Family who brought change. You will be a leader. But what about Cass?"

What was Charity talking about? Cass would be there with him, advancing their studies, helping people, saving the world. Right?

Realization dawned on him. But was that something she wanted? And would society accept someone like Cass?

Charity was watching him. "Those questions are worth pondering," she said quietly. "For your sake and for Cass's."

"I haven't thought that far," Theo conceded. "We don't have much time left with what we're doing now. There might not even be a world left in a couple weeks. At least for most of us."

Charity nodded. "That is true." She stood. "Theo, please forgive my pertinence." A slight smile appeared on her face. "Perhaps I have something in common with Cass, speaking my thoughts out loud. At least with people I am comfortable with."

That would explain why Charity was usually quiet at the business meetings. "I always appreciate your candor, Charity."

Charity's smile filtered into serious eyes. "Maybe if we live through this, and there is a new world on the other side of it all, that world doesn't need to be the same as this one."

"Miss Charity." The maid looked in. "The guest rooms are ready."

Charity glance at Theo. "Why don't you get settled. We can talk more later."

Theo was relieved. "That would be nice."

The conversation had been getting uncomfortable.

21

THEO FINISHED TYING THE CUFFS OF HIS SHIRT AND straightened the vest the maid had brought him. It felt good to have the last two weeks washed away. He brushed back his damp hair, checked the mirror one more time, then left the guest room and headed down the hall.

The wood paneling and soft green wallpaper made the house feel peaceful. Theo paused next to the window near the grand staircase and looked out. The backyard ended at the edge of the floating city, with the Mist and skyline stretching beyond as far as the eye could see. An iron-wrought fence lined the edge to keep a clumsy stumble from proving fatal. The rest of the yard was a beautiful garden, sectioned off in squares with bright-red tomatoes, leafy potato plants, carrots, and squash. There was even a beehive in one corner. Three fruit trees stood next to the fence, and a handful of chickens clucked and pecked at insects in the garden.

Adora would love this place. He leaned against the window. He missed his sister. He missed his home. He missed his way of life. The last two weeks had been more difficult than he would like to admit. But he was stronger for it.

A noise downstairs drew his attention. He reached the top

stair and looked down. Cass stood near the front door, dressed in a simple blouse and long brown skirt. Her rose-gold hair hung in damp curls along her back. He stood gazing a little longer than he intended.

"I'm glad to see my father's clothes fit, although a bit looser on your frame."

Charity came up to him, and a flush crept up his neck. "Yes, thank you." Had she seen him staring at Cass?

At the same moment, Cass glanced up the stairs.

Theo tugged on his collar as he descended and spoke to Cass. "I figure we should visit Eli Gresley tonight, that way his debt is satisfied and I'm free to use the crew. Maybe even to use the ship name."

"How will we leave without Luron noticing if he is out there?" Cass asked.

"You will use my zipper," Charity intervened. "The landing pad is around back. If you fly past the edge of Decadenn, then circle back into the city, it should throw anyone off who might be following you. You do know how to fly?"

"Yes."

Charity led them to the back of the house. "Where are you going, by the way?"

"Grime Row."

She thought for a moment. "There is a place to land on the northern side of Grime Row. Go past the steel buildings to where the older part of Decadenn is. It's the only landing pad in that part of the city, so you can't miss it."

Charity went left and out a side door. Just beyond the door and near the gardens stood a brass zipper on a round-shaped landing pavement near a small hangar.

Theo approached it. "It's similar to my zipper, so there shouldn't be any problems." He checked everything, then opened the door for Cass before proceeding around the zipper.

He sat down and peered at the panel. "And the instruments are the same." He looked at Cass. "Ready to go?"

Cass settled inside the zipper. "Yes. It's been too long since I've felt the wind on my face." Theo grinned and handed her a pair of goggles. He shot Charity a look of gratitude. She nodded and stepped back. He worked the knobs, checked the instruments, then started the zipper.

The wings on either side responded with a sudden whizzing sound as they started to flap at an unbelievable speed. Cass held onto the side and marveled at their blur.

Seconds later, the zipper rose. Theo cleared the house and trees, and then went past the yard, past the iron fence, and out across the Mist. He brought the zipper around and started circling the city. From this vantage point, Decadenn looked amazing.

Suddenly Cass laughed.

Theo glanced over at her.

"This is amazing," she shouted, her hair sailing behind her.

Yes, it was. Theo grinned and the zipper sped forward.

They circled a quarter of the city, then he turned the zipper and started in toward the buildings. They flew over towers of steel and metal, belching smokestacks, and paved streets far below.

As they approached the older section of the city, marked by a change from steel to brick, a large paved circle appeared below where streets broke off like spokes. Theo started their descent. There was one other zipper parked there, a more golden color.

Gently he brought their zipper down, lower, lower, until it settled with a slight bump onto the landing pad. He turned the engine off and removed his goggles. "So do you like flying in a zipper or gliding more?"

Cass removed her own goggles and shook her curls out. "Both," she said with a grin. She ran a hand through her hair and then gestured at it helplessly. "It's pretty wild, isn't it?"

Before he could think, Theo reached over and tugged on a curl. "I like it this way." His stomach did a weird flip, and they stared at each other, her eyes wide and as green as emeralds, his heart racing like an overheated engine. He dropped the curl as if it were on fire.

Cass scrambled out of the zipper, her face as red as his felt. "Which one is Grime Row? Once we are on the street, I think I can steer us to Eli's pawn shop."

"Pawn shop?"

Cass looked back at him. "Yes, he owns a pawn shop."

He put the goggles away. "I've never been in one."

"First time for everything."

"That is true." His mind flickered to the curl. He'd never done that before, with any woman. He shook himself and looked around. He spotted a sign posted at the corner of one of the streets. "There it is. Grime Row."

Cass led the way. Grime Row was less of a street and more of a shadowed gap between towering buildings. The further they went, the darker it became, with trash strewn along the brick walls and dingy doorways. After a couple of blocks, Cass stopped in front of a small wooden door with three golden globes suspended from a rod overhead.

As they opened the door, a bell rang inside. Theo ducked his head and entered behind Cass. Copper pipes crisscrossed the low ceiling, and gas lamps flickered across the walls, barely lighting the room. A wooden counter ran along the left side, while the right side was stacked from floor to ceiling with various pieces of furniture, a handful of paintings, a gilded mirror, and a brass birdcage. He also spotted a couple old snuffboxes, a jewelry box, and other knickknacks. What a strange collection of items.

"Hello?" Cass called out as she walked past the wooden counter. "Mr. Gresley, are you here?"

Just as she reached the back, where a door stood ajar, the door swung open and a long, lean man appeared. His shirt collar was unbuttoned, and the fabric was wrinkled as if he had slept in it. His eyes focused in on Theo. He didn't seem to notice Cass at all as he walked right by her.

"Hello, sir," the man said, smoothing his shirt and fastening the last button. "Forgive me, I seemed to have dozed off in back. How can I help you today? Looking for something particular?" There was a greedy glint in his gaze that set Theo on guard immediately.

"You're Eli Gresley, owner of the *Daedalus*?"

The man's face darkened. "I am. But I'm afraid the ship is not available right now." He finally noticed Cass, and his eyes went wide. "You! You're one of Victor's divers, the one that agreed to work off the debt." He went up to Cass and towered over her. "Where have you all been? Thought you could just run off and disappear, you little rat!"

Cass stared at him defiantly. "I didn't run. Why do you think I'm here now?"

"She's with me," Theo said, stepping between them. "And I am here to take care of the *Daedalus's* debt."

Eli looked at them both, then focused on Theo. "Who are you exactly?" he said, his simpering attitude gone.

"Theodore Winchester, of the Winchester family."

"Winchester? As in one of the House of Lords?"

"The one and the same."

"I see." The greedy glint was back. "Then let's talk."

The longer he was in Eli's presence, the more Theo disliked the man. If anyone was a rat in this room, it was Eli. "I've talked to Bert, the former captain—" he held up a hand when Eli opened his mouth. "I know what happened to the *Daedalus*, and I know how much is left to be paid. I will do that and no more."

Eli folded his arms. "Why are you paying for a ship that no longer exists?"

"Because I want the name and business of the *Daedalus*. And the crew."

Eli gave a harsh laugh. "The agreement I made was with Bert and her. Not with you."

"But like you said, no one is going to pay for a ship that no longer exists."

"She will." Eli turned and gave Cass his full attention. He looked her over, and Theo barely held back the sudden urge to punch Eli's face. "After all, this little lady and Bert gave me their word."

Theo breathed in through his nostrils. "But without a ship, you know they can't pay you back."

"There are other ways. I could have them Purged."

"What?" Cass stepped right up to Eli and glared into his face. "You're disgusting. And dishonest. You are nothing like your brother! You are a greedy, wretched man. You don't deserve the Gresley name, you—"

Theo grabbed Cass and pulled her back. He looked Eli full in the face. "No, you can't. You can do nothing. Nothing at all. I have the full power and authority of my family name, and I will use it against you. I would not only see your little shop razed, I would see to it every sterling you have was taxed until you have nothing left." His voice grew low and cold. "So you have no choice. You take my offer. I will pay what is left of the debt Bert and Cass owe you. Or you lose everything. What will it be?"

Eli stood absolutely still, regarding Theo as if gauging how serious he was. Theo stared right back. He was serious. Very serious.

Eli seemed to get the hint. "Fine." He shrugged. "I'll take your offer."

"Good idea. I will have payment drawn up in your name at

the Bank of Decadenn tomorrow for the amount Bert told me. In exchange, you will release the *Daedalus* title, the business, and the crew. And I want it in writing."

"Right now?"

"Yes. We will wait."

Eli muttered under his breath. "Give me five minutes." He turned and exited through the back door.

Theo kept his eyes on the door, his whole body rigid, until he felt Cass take his hand. Then everything left him like a gust of air.

"You were brilliant," she said.

"Apparently Captain Gresley wasn't anything like his brother."

Cass's eyes sparked. "The complete opposite. He was the smartest, kindest, most generous man I'd ever met. If not for him, I don't know where I'd be today." Her hand slipped from his. "I'd probably be dead."

"I wish I could have met him."

Cass smiled sadly. "Me too."

They waited in the stillness, exhausted by all that had transpired that day. Theo rolled his shoulders. Tomorrow he would have the check drawn. Then hopefully they would hear back from Professor Hawkins and have a ship. Then . . .

He looked over at Cass as she fingered a birdcage nearby. Charity's words rang in his ears: *a fourth of Tyromourne has disappeared.* How many more cities were disappearing into the Mist? He heard Eli returning. They didn't have much time.

Please, Elaeros. Let Cass have the cure we need.

22

THEO PAUSED OVER THE WASHBASIN THE NEXT morning, his face dripping. Go to the bank, secure the check for Eli—he glared at the opaque water as he thought of the pawnbroker—then see if Bert had found a ship.

He reached for the towel and wiped his face. He glanced at the nearby window. Another bright and beautiful day, with a blue sky and white, billowy clouds. Each day was a gift, even more so with the rising combined threat of the Mist and the Five Families. He would not take even an hour for granted. He closed his eyes, let out a long breath, and prayed.

Cass was already dressed and out in the hallway when he emerged. "Good morning, Cass."

She spun around. "Good morning, Theo."

"Would you like to go to the bank with me?"

Her face lit up. "Yes." She lowered her voice. "I can only stay inside for so long before I become restless."

Theo laughed. He wasn't surprised. "Then let's go."

They headed to the back of the house where the zipper was parked. Charity had given him permission to use it while he was here, and it seemed like a better option than traveling by steamshuttle, where they would be more out in the open and potentially spotted. No doubt by now Luron had figured out where they were. But the less he knew of their comings and goings, the better. Although Theo was still puzzled as to why the masked man hadn't approached them yet. Perhaps Charity was right and with the bluecoats under their jurisdiction, neither Luron nor the Staggs Family would draw near them here.

They once again took to the air. Theo kept glancing at Cass from the corner of his eye. The joy he saw on her face washed over him and spread across his own. Twenty minutes later, he looped the zipper around toward an enormous three-story stone building.

The Bank of Decadenn took up a whole block, its architecture from the time before the Mist. Every detail of the building exuded wealth and power, from the wide staircase to the oak double doors and narrow, arched windows. Pillars held the portico up above the stairs, giving the entrance a grand feel.

Theo brought the zipper down on the circular pad, located on the other side of the street, and turned off the engine. A few pedestrians glanced their way and gave Theo a cursory nod. They were part of the wealthy class, given their attire and proximity to the bank. Only those with money had any business at the depository.

What a stark contrast to Grime Row and Eli's shop.

He secured the zipper and his goggles, stepped around the vehicle, and opened the passenger door. Cass didn't move.

"Are you coming?" he asked.

She shook herself as if coming out of a reverie. She placed the goggles away and emerged. All the joy and excitement during the trip here seemed to have fled.

"Cass, are you alright?"

Her eyes were glued to the building before them. "That's the bank?"

"Yes."

He moved to her side and took her arm. She didn't seem to notice. After waiting for a cargo cart to pass by, they crossed the street and headed up the staircase. Cass remained silent. At the doors, he reached for the right one and held it open for her.

She sucked in her breath in the doorway and gripped his arm tighter. Theo gently steered her into the lobby.

The inside of the bank was as magnificent as the outside. Golden chandeliers hung high above, twinkling against the paneled ceiling. Deep, rich wood paneling lined the walls and floor, and red wallpaper with golden ivy covered the upper half of the room. A grand staircase led to the second floor, where more private transactions took place. Along one wall was a row of booths where clerks attended customers. The other side, beneath windows enclosed in golden brocade curtains, were desks and lamps with globe-like lights.

"I—uh—I think I might wait outside," Cass said, voice uncharacteristically small.

Theo glanced down at her. She appeared pale in the light. "Are you sure? Maybe we can come back later. You seem ill."

She let go of his arm and stepped away. "I'm not ill. I just—" she glanced around. "It's a bit too much for me."

He looked around again, seeing the opulence and affluence through her eyes. He was used to such places—she was not. "Of course. I can come back another time."

Cass stopped him. "No, go ahead and conduct your business. I'll wait outside."

Before he could protest, she left. Theo watched after her. Should he follow her? No. She would want him to finish what he was here to do. Theo headed for the staircase. It wouldn't take long to have a check drawn up for Eli, and another one ready for Bert—if he'd been able to secure a ship. Then Theo would rejoin Cass outside.

23

NEVER HAD SHE FELT SO OUT OF PLACE AS SHE DID just now. Cass breathed in the outside air as she stood at the top of the staircase, then fled down. It brought back a flash of memories of her time on the streets, when she'd been run off, hostile shouts following her.

She slowed a bit, then walked quickly along the street. She had no idea where she was going, only that she needed to get away. After a block, the tight band around her chest began to loosen. Another block, and a light wind brushed her face and swept her curls back. Slowly, a weight she had only vaguely been aware of carrying for the last few weeks started to lift from her shoulders, and she felt a sense of freedom. For all of the beauty and modern conveniences that came with grand houses, tearooms, and stately buildings, they were nothing compared to the outdoors.

Cass paused beneath the shade of a towering tree that stood on the corner. From her vantage point, she could still see the front of the bank and watch for Theo without being noticed. And the shade brought a reprieve from the ever-warming summer rays.

The street was busy with pedestrians, and Cass watched

them with mixed emotions. There was no hint of fear among the people passing by, unlike Belhold. Was that because there was very little panic here over the rising Mist? She wasn't sure of the altitude, but it was possible Decadenn might be beyond the Mist's reach.

Two men, deep in discussion and dressed in fine clothing and top hats, approached.

"The port master wants to close Decadenn to refugees."

"Refugees from the mountain cities?"

"Yes. And I agree with him. If we let one group in, they'll all flock here."

"But don't we have a duty to help those trying to escape the Mist?"

"We have a duty to our city and our people first. And it's not Decadenn's job to find a solution, it's the House of Lords'."

The conversation drifted away as they passed. Cass clenched her hands. The attitude of one was calloused, and the worries of the other were shallow.

Would the world change if something within her blood made it possible for all people to survive the Mist? Or would people always look out for themselves first and foremost?

Her conscience pricked her. She wasn't really any different. For years she focused on her own survival. Then she met the crew of the *Daedalus*. Now . . .

She was learning what it meant to help others. Really help them. Like the way Captain Gresley helped each crewmember by taking them aboard the *Daedalus*. And Theo, who was willing to put not only his position but his life at risk for everyone, not just his peers—

A glint of gold caught her eye.

Cass stilled. There. A block away to her right, outside a narrow brick building with a sign swinging over the door, stood Luron, dressed exactly like the two gentleman who had just passed by—his top hat in place, cane in his hand. The exception was the golden mask over his face.

She glanced around, then slipped past the tree and into a narrow alley behind her. Her heart raced. Had he seen her? She didn't think so. But what was he doing here? He stood near the post building. Was he sending a message? Reporting to his superiors? What should she do?

Cass waited, her back pressed against a stone wall, the air feeling cooler than it had a couple minutes ago. Part of her wanted Theo to quickly finish his business so they could flee before Luron found them. And part of her wanted him to take a while, so Luron would be gone by the time Theo came out. Meanwhile, she would stay here, out of sight—

"There you are," said a raspy voice.

Cass froze as Luron appeared in the gap between the buildings, blocking her way to the street.

"What a coincidence meeting you here. I have been hoping to see you privately, without your guard dog." The sarcasm in his voice revealed the encounter to be no coincidence.

She furtively eyed the area, looking for a way of escape. "What do you want with me?"

"I want to talk."

She looked up at him. The metal mask covered his features, with a triangle slit for his nose, two holes for his mouth, and dark ovals for eyes. What did he hide behind it? She tried not to shudder. "About what?"

"The future."

She noticed a small gap to his right, where she might possibly squeeze through. A saber and revolver hung beneath his overcoat. He seemed to sense what she was thinking because he took a sidestep, effectively blocking her.

"No leaving until we talk."

"About what? I know who you work for. And I'm not

interested in anything that has to do with the Staggs."

He laughed, but it was not a nice laugh. "You're wrong," he said, his voice even more raspy. "I work only for myself. Right now, my goals align with the echelon family. But soon that will change." His use of the derogatory term surprised her. "I believe we are alike. Neither of us Turn in the Mist. Yet we are treated only like vermin by those above us."

Cass stared. "How do you know I don't Turn?"

The head tilted. "I saw you that day. No mask. And I've dug into your past. You were once a street rat, escaping the Purges until you were hired on as a diver on the *Daedalus*."

How did he know all of this? Her heart beat faster. She was sure no one knew of her past save Theo and the *Daedalus* crew. The House of Lords couldn't possibly be that informed.

He held out a gloved hand and brushed his finger along her chin. "You're just like me."

Cass flinched at his touch. "I don't know you apart from the fact that you work for the Five Families. You are just saying that to gain my sympathy."

"Alright. That is a fair point." He lifted his hand to his head. A moment later, something clicked, and his mask swung to the side, exposing a face so scarred it looked barely human. His nose was missing, and his lips were gone, leaving behind a slit for his mouth. The rest of his face was red and pink with white, narrow ridges.

Cass swallowed and jerked her gaze away.

"As you can see, they once tried to Purge me," his voice rasped. "Just like they Purge everyone they deem below them. In the fire, I discovered I was different. I was meant to live, despite these scars and wounds. I was chosen by the Mist. And so were you." He brought the mask back around, and Cass heard the plate clasp back into place. "Do not think for one moment my allegiance lies with those who did this to me."

She swallowed again. She would never forget that face. Wretched and scarred. But chosen by the Mist? He was not sane.

"Let me ask you something: do you think the world will change once the Mist disappears?"

Cass stared at the stone wall, still unable to look at him, despite the mask being back in place. He had just voiced her own thoughts from minutes ago. Her silence confirmed his perceptions. "I see you don't think the world will change, either."

She wanted to spin around and deny it right then and there, but seeing his face, and remembering the night her parents were Purged brought back all those terrible feelings she had carried before she joined the *Daedalus*. No, she didn't believe the world would change. The powerful would still oppress the weak, those with means would take from the destitute, and people would continue to suffer.

"What if we let the world start over?" Luron leaned into her and she bent back.

"What do you mean?"

"Let the Mist do what it was meant to do. Let it cover the world, and let a new way of life begin."

"Are you saying everyone should be left to die, and I . . . I go off with you?" She couldn't believe what she was hearing. The idea was ludicrous.

"Yes."

He truly was insane. She tried to hide her revulsion. "How is that any different than the Purges?"

"Because instead of humans choosing who lives or dies, nature will."

He was serious. This madman was proposing they go off and live in the Mist and let the rest of humankind perish. A shiver rippled down her spine. She was dealing with a lunatic.

And yet . . . and yet there was something in her that did agree with what he said. What if the world could start over? No more echelons and scroungers. No more Purges and pain and heartache.

But was more death really the answer?

Luron tipped his head toward her in a deferential manner. "Do not answer now. Think about what I've said. What world do you want to save? We will meet again, and I will ask you one more time. Your answer will have consequences."

She watched him leave and realized she was trembling. She stood in the alley for a while, near the large tree, his words playing in her mind. She noted the post again. Why had he gone there? Maybe she could find out.

Cass left the alley after making sure Luron was gone. She crossed the street and pushed the post door open. A small bell rang as she entered.

A long wooden counter stood on the left, with matching wood cubicles that lined two walls from floor to ceiling. Brown-paper parcels, stacks of envelopes, and baskets filled the cubbyholes.

Cass stood on her tiptoes and looked over the counter. The postmaster knelt on the floor, tying a bit of twine around a large box.

"Excuse me."

The man looked up. "I'm sorry, miss, I didn't hear you enter." He stood and brushed off his dark-blue uniform. His mustache was oiled and his dark hair captured beneath a cap.

"I have a question."

"Yes, miss?"

"That man who was here not too long ago—the one with a golden mask—is there a chance I could find out if he was sending a post? And, if so, to where he sent it?"

He pushed up his cap and scratched his temple as he looked her over.

Cass suppressed the urge to swallow. *I'm a lady, I'm a lady,* she chanted inside her mind while she stood still, hoping her clothes would convince him.

"I'm sorry, miss," he finally said. "I can't divulge that information."

"Oh." Of course he couldn't. What was she thinking?

"Is there anything else I can do for you? Send a post? Deliver a package?"

She gave him the best smile she could muster. "No, that will be all."

"Alright, miss. You have a good day." And he seemed to mean it.

"You too."

If by chance Luron was in communication with the Staggs, why hadn't they taken action yet? Was it because Luron wanted to speak to her first for his own purposes?

Outside, a hollow feeling spread through her chest. She pressed her hand against the spot.

Luron's words haunted her, twisting and worming their way into the deep recess of her mind. Before, her only goal had been survival. But now there ran within her veins a very real possibility of saving everyone from the Mist.

But if nothing changed, was it worth saving the world?

24

THE BLUECOATS NEVER CAME TO THE ATWOOD manse. Theo wasn't sure if that was because Luron's mission was simply observation or due to the Atwood's connection with the captain. In any case, he was thankful for a day of rest.

There was a knock on his door. Theo opened it to find Edgar standing in the hall with a thick note in his hand.

"This arrived just now, sir." He held the note out.

Theo's spirits rose. A reply from Professor Hawkins. And it appeared to be a lengthy one. "Thank you, Edgar," he said. He shut the door and went to the chair near the window, his eyes glued to the front of the missive. This was it. Now they would know for sure.

He carefully undid the twine and broke the seal. Five pages with tiny scrawling letters and illustrations. The further he read, the faster his heart beat. It was more than he had hoped. He didn't quite understand all of Professor Hawkins's words, but what he did understand was that they could utilize Cass's blood. Not only that, but the solution would be fairly simple and easy to distribute.

Theo shot to his feet and suppressed the urge to let out a whoop.

He thought of his parents, and his eyes teared up as he reread the letter. "We did it," he whispered. Professor Hawkins requested another sample, but that would be easy. And if Bert had found a ship, they could sail back to Belhold as soon as it was ready.

He lowered the letter, the pervading seriousness of the situation hitting him more deeply. Luron was watching and reporting to the Staggs Family. Belhold was under the Staggs and Kingsford jurisdiction. And even though Margaret Etherington was in Tyromourne, he wasn't sure where that family stood. Had the rising Mist changed her mind, or was she as stubborn as ever?

They had the Atwoods on their side, or at least Charity. He needed to let her know. And he wanted to talk to Reynard. Charity had said her father would be home this evening. Theo knew they'd need all the help they could get.

But his first thought was Cass, and he found her a few minutes later, facing away from him, standing outside the iron fence that surrounded the Atwood property. Beyond, the Mist lay like a greenish-grey sea with nothing but blue sky above.

He held up the letter and waved it as he ran. "It came!"

Cass turned around. She was back to wearing her trousers and tunic with a set of boots. Her leather corset held everything in place, and the only thing missing were her tools and her goggles. Her reddish gold curls fluttered around her face in the breeze. "News from your professor?"

Theo smiled, slightly out of breath. "Yes."

"Did they discover something?"

"Yes! Just as was predicted, the blood of those immune to the Bioformin can be used to inoculate the rest of the population with the same immunity."

Cass looked at him, eyebrow raised.

Theo chuckled at her expression. "I admit the language is a bit dense."

Cass glanced at the letter. "So, in your own words, what exactly does the blood do, and how can it help other people?"

Theo folded the paper. "This is what I understand. Blood carries the spores to the brain and Turns a person. It was an unknown side effect when the Bioformin was created. But your blood does not carry the spores; therefore, they never reach the brain. Professor Hawkins spoke with his colleagues, and they believe they have devised a way to mimic what your blood does. But they need more samples, fresh samples. Which means we need to head back to Belhold."

"Belhold," she said quietly.

"I know it's risky. We have no idea what the Staggs or the other Families might have planned. And with Luron here communicating with them, it'll be hard to find a way back without being detected. If there were a way to send Professor Hawkins what he needs, I would do that instead. But he and his colleagues need a fresh sample. Maybe more than one. I'm not sure exactly how they will duplicate your immunity and expand its use."

"I'm not afraid of the risk." But there was uncertainty in her face.

"You know the *Daedalus* crew and I will do everything we can to get you to Belhold safely. In many ways, the fate of humanity is at stake."

She looked away. "I know."

Theo watched her, trying to figure out what she was thinking. He thought she'd be jubilant. "Cass," he said quietly. When she didn't respond, he gently grasped her wrist. Her pulse was racing beneath his fingertips. "I can feel your heartbeat." She looked up at him and something moved inside his chest. "I see fear in your eyes."

She gave him a small nod.

That's all it took. Theo pulled her to him and wrapped his arms around her. He felt her tense, then relax against him. No, more than that. She clung to him and buried her head in his sweater, holding him tightly.

Seconds later, she looked up at him. "Thank you," she said, her voice heavy with emotion. "I think I needed that."

He gave her a soft smile. "You looked like you did." He lifted his hand and brushed her cheek. "Cass?"

"Yes?"

His heart was bursting with some unnamed emotion, something that wanted to wrap this young woman up and keep her safe. "May I kiss you?"

Her eyes went wide. But there was something in them . . .

Before he could say anything, Cass reached up and gave him a quick kiss on the lips, then spun around and dashed inside the Atwood manse.

Theo remained where he was and watched her disappear, still feeling the slight brush of her mouth against his. Charity was right. There *was* a bond between them. One he would fight for. No line of demarcation between echelons and scrounger. Just human beings. Together.

25

CASS PRESSED A HAND TO HER FACE AND CLOSED her eyes. *What was I thinking? Kissing Theodore Byron Winchester, of the Five Families!*

"Good morning, Cass."

Cass whirled around to find Charity standing in the doorway to the front room. "Good morning."

"Are you feeling well? You look flush."

"Yes. It's just hot out today."

Before anything more was said, Cass excused herself and hurried to the guest room. After shutting the door, she stood stock still in the middle of the room.

I kissed him. Yes, it was hardly anything, but it was enough to send her heart flying. She'd never kissed anyone before, not even her parents.

A thought pierced her momentary happiness. If she cared that much about Theo, why did she hesitate to tell him about her talk with Luron? The conversation came back to her in full. She was ashamed of the thoughts she had afterwards. A good person would want to save others.

Maybe . . . maybe I'm not a good person.

For years her only goal had been to stay alive. There was no room to debate the idea of good or bad. Life just was. But every time she thought about those who lived along the upper tiers of Belhold, about their words and scorn, a fire filled her gut.

Like it did now.

She wasn't afraid of the possible upcoming risks. It wasn't fear at all. It was a clash between a lifetime of hurt and her heart. How to save the world. Including those people who never cared about her and allowed the Purges to happen.

She let out a long, heavy breath. *I don't have an answer yet.* But she would need to. Soon.

CASS AND THEO ARRIVED BACK AT DECADENN'S PORT a half hour after receiving Bert's message.

Theo pulled the message from his pocket. "Bert said he's waiting with a possible ship at Dock E."

Cass peeked at the sign hanging on the post along the walkway. "We're at F, so it's only one dock away." She couldn't help but notice Theo gazed at her differently now. She found it secretly delightful.

They reached the dock and turned down the walkway. Cass stopped as her eyes caught sight of the ship waiting for them. It was smaller than the *Daedalus*, but with sleeker lines and polished wood. Instead of an oval airbag, this one was a sphere, with pulleys and ropes wrapped around it so it could be accessed easier. A row of windows encased the lower stern, where the captain's cabin would be, and portholes surrounded the rest of the lower decks. A large crane stood in the middle of the ship, a perfect contraption for bringing loot up from the Mist.

"It's amazing," Cass breathed.

"You like it?"

She nodded. "Yes."

Theo smiled at her. "Then let's see if we can acquire it."

As they approached the gangplank, Bert emerged at the top of the ship. Another man was with him, portly with a bald head and bright-colored clothes. Bert spotted them and waved them up.

As they walked up the plank, Cass took in all the details of the ship. There were hooks for the ropes, and nets to hold cargo along the top deck, which would make sense since the ship was smaller and thus had a smaller hold. At the top, she ran her hand along the wooden railing. No nicks or splinters and perfectly polished. If the ship became theirs, its pristine state wouldn't last very long after a couple trips, but she would certainly enjoy it in the meantime. Hopefully.

Bert came forward. "Cass, Mr. Winchester, it's good to see you both."

Cass's head snapped up at Theo's formal name.

The shorter man rubbed his hands together. "Ah, Mister Winchester. It is nice to meet you. Let me introduce myself. Amos Massey at your service."

Theo's face darkened. "Yes, I've heard of you."

"Good, good." Amos didn't seem to catch Theo's expression. Cass watched the two of them with interest.

"Your friend here tells me that you wish to purchase this fine ship."

"I am in the market for a ship," Theo acknowledged. He crossed his arms. "Tell me why I should buy yours."

The man began to rattle off a number of details. Cass nodded in appreciation. Good engine, practical but beautiful, and fast. And with a fully decked out captain's cabin. Not that she'd be allowed to stay in such a room, but someday, if she could earn enough money to have her own ship . . .

"So why are you selling such a fine vessel?"

"There is a great demand now for ships, what with the Mist rising and all." Amos's teeth gleamed.

"Why not keep it for yourself?"

Amos shrugged. "I have two others. When Bert told me one of the Five Families was in the market for a ship, I wanted to help out."

Cass leaned in. "So how much are you asking?"

"Ah, getting down to business now. Fifty thousand sterlings."

Fifty . . . thousand? Cass felt weak.

Theo's reply startled her. "This ship is worth more than that. Why so little?"

"Let's just say I want to be on your good side, Mister Winchester. Remember the Massey name."

"So a favor."

Amos shrugged again. "Something like that."

Theo took another look around the ship. He regarded Amos for a moment. Finally, he said, "I'll take it."

Cass watched in stunned amazement as Theo pulled out an ivory piece of paper. Once again she was reminded of how rich Theo was. To be able to pay a man fifty thousand sterlings without blinking an eye and buy a ship right then and there.

"I want the ship today," Theo stated.

"Yes, of course." Amos flashed his teeth again. "I'll have everything arranged within the hour."

Theo looked over at Bert who had stood silently off to the side this whole time. "Will the crew be ready to sail?"

"We will need to familiarize ourselves with the ship, but we should be able to head out today," he responded.

"Good," Theo nodded. "There is something important to be done that requires us to leave as soon as possible. Let me know if you need me to do anything."

"I will."

Though Bert kept his voice crisp, Cass could feel his elation.

She began to walk the perimeter of the main deck while Theo finished the transaction with Amos. Her fingers trailed along the railing, heart swelling with love and pride for this ship, even though it wasn't hers. It was the most beautiful thing she'd ever seen.

Several minutes later, a figure fell beside her, and she glanced up. "So what are we going to name this ship?" Theo asked.

Cass already knew. "It's the *Daedalus* reborn."

"So you want to name it the *Daedalus*?"

She gave a firm nod. "I would if it were my ship. The *Daedalus II*, but," she said, "I would shorten it to the *Daedalus*."

Theo laughed. "Alright."

She cocked her head. Was he serious? "So you're really going to name the ship that?"

"Unless you want me to name it the *Cassiopeia*."

"What? No, definitely no!"

"Are you sure?" His eyes danced at her. "It's not every day you have a chance to have a ship named after you."

"I think I'll pass."

"Alright then. *Daedalus* it is."

Cass's heart sang. No matter what, she would stay on as the crew as long as Theo would have her. After all, she was one of the best divers out there.

THERE WOULD BE A DELAY BEFORE THE NAME WAS painted along the side of the sleek vessel. Right now, they were needed back in Belhold. A two-week trip loomed ahead of them, if good weather held out.

Cass hummed that same tune Theo was always humming,

checking out every corner of the new ship. Bert had secured four gliders and masks, and once they were back in Belhold, she would go retrieve the gear she and Theo had left behind in the textile factory. More samples of her blood would be taken, and Theo's group could perform whatever scientific wonder they needed to do.

A shadow entered her heart as she inspected the galley, the same shadow from that morning. If she were honest, the only people she had the deepest desire to save were her people. Those who had suffered along the dead zone. The ones who were Purged. The shadow deepened as she stared at the new pots waiting on the counter and the handful of pans hanging on hooks. Patterson would not be making this trip with them.

A tear came unbidden to her eye, and she quickly brushed it away. She would miss the gruff old man. Another casualty of the Five Families.

No. She shook her head. Not all of them. Not Theo. And not Charity. But it didn't seem fair that the Staggs family and others would benefit from her blood, despite how hard they were trying to stop anything from happening. They would still have their homes, and unless something drastic happened, they would still govern the people. Anger lit inside her. If only she could select who received the cure.

No.

She sat down on the bench and glanced out the nearby porthole. That wasn't right. What was she thinking?

She clenched her hand across the newly polished table. Outside the galley, she could hear the crew talking and preparing for flight. Her thoughts came back from that morning. *I'm not a good person.*

Cass stared in front of her. *How does Theo find the fortitude to be so kind? Is it his belief in Elaeros?* It was the same with Captain Gresley. Two men who exuded hope and saw light in the future. And not only that, took the hands of others and brought them forward.

She swallowed hard. *I want to be like that, Elaeros.* More tears came to her eyes. *But I don't know how.*

She sat there, her head bowed, a war raging again inside her chest. She lifted her eyes and stared at the porthole ahead. A subtle shift moved inside her, as if she had crossed some invisible line.

She let out a breath she didn't realize she had been holding. "Elaeros," she said again, this time aloud. More than her feelings, more than the hurt, she wanted to follow Elaeros. And this was her first step.

Here I am. Use me.

26

MID-AFTERNOON THE *DAEDALUS II* LEFT DECADENN.
Cass stood on the bow with Bert and Theo, wearing a grin that
would not leave her face. The warm air pressed against her
cheeks as the ship started eastward, and the sun blazed down
across her shoulders. It was a hot summer day, but she didn't
care—they were flying again. She looked up at the bright blue
sky, and her heart soared. This was where she belonged.

After an hour, the crew settled into routine tasks. Cass
worked with Will in the engine room as they familiarized
themselves with the new motor. The bell rang, signaling dinner.
Bert had brought a new cook on board, a lean young man barely
taller than Cass, with thick black curls that stuck up around his
face and with the darkest eyes she had ever seen.

"Hi, Owen," Cass said with a bright smile as she reached for
the bowl of soup he held out to her.

"H-hi," he said as his cheeks flushed.

"This smells delicious! Thank you." She took the bowl and
headed for the table next to the porthole. A few moments later,
Theo sat down across from her with his own steaming bowl.

"You're going to scare poor Owen with your exuberance,"
Theo said with a laugh.

"What?"

"After you left, the young man was so dazed it took me saying his name three times for him to realize I was standing there. I don't think he's quite sure how to respond to a female diver."

She grinned. "He'll have to get used to it." She swallowed a spoonful. Mmmm. Bert had chosen a good cook. Chicken, potatoes, and a few carrots in a thickened broth. Whatever magic Owen had performed, it tasted like heaven in a bowl.

She glanced at Theo. "So what was that between you and Amos this morning?" she asked between bites.

"You mean the leech who sold us this ship?" Theo actually snorted. "He's well known, always clinging to the Five Families, trying to obtain favors. I didn't realize he was in Decadenn. Last time I heard about him, he was in Belhold trying to gain a tenant landlord position from the Kingsford Family. I wonder how he purchased this ship. But I checked with Bert, and all the paperwork is sound."

"I've known people like him." Cass shook her head. Then smiled. "But I do love this ship. I'm glad it's yours now."

Theo looked like he was going to say something, but then shook his head. She waited, but he only went back to eating.

Cass dismissed her curiosity. But she did want to know what the captain's cabin looked like. It was the only area of the ship she hadn't explored. But it was Theo's room, and she had no business in there. A partition had been set up in the crew's quarters for her use. Bert had hung long strips of canvas from the ceiling, leaving an area just big enough for her hammock and space beneath for a small chest she could keep her belongings in. She missed the small room she had occupied on the original *Daedalus*, but if it meant flying on this beautiful ship, she'd even sleep on the deck.

As Cass finished her last spoonful, she found Theo watching her. "Cass, can we meet this evening?"

Her heart sped up. "You mean just the two of us?"

Theo looked puzzled, then a smile flashed across his face before growing serious again. "A handful of us. Bert, Cyrus, Jeremiah. I want to be prepared for anything. If Luron has been communicating with the Staggs family, then there's a chance they'll be waiting for us near Belhold."

Cass almost coughed. She never did tell Theo about her meeting with Luron. But did it matter now? If she ran into him again, she knew her answer. That information would only worry Theo. "Of course. I don't have the night watch tonight."

"We will meet in my cabin at seven."

She dropped the bowl off at the counter and headed out to the deck. There was a small part of her that wished Theo just wanted to meet with her. She missed their alone times together.

What would happen when this was all over? She would remain on this ship as long as she could, but what would become of her and Theo? Would they remain friends when the Mist was no longer a threat? Or would they go their separate ways?

CASS CAUGHT HER BREATH WHEN SHE ENTERED THE captain's cabin that night. It was just as she had imagined and so much more. The room was absolutely beautiful. Wood panels lining the walls matched the floor. Thick, curved wooden beams held the ceiling up. An array of windows encased the far wall with a view of night sky. Lit hurricane lamps hung along the ceiling beams, filling the area with a soft and comforting light.

The furniture matched the wooden panels. A desk sat against the left wall with built-in bookcases on either side. A double bed, topped with a scarlet cover and fluffy pillows, rested below the windows. A large chest sat at the foot of the bed for storage. To the right, a painting of a sunset hung on the wall above four chairs and a table.

Jeremiah entered the cabin with a low whistle. "Nice room," he said as he made his way to one of the chairs around the table. Cass took the seat next to him as Bert and Cyrus entered. Bert stayed on his feet while Cyrus sat across from Jeremiah. Cass's only time with Cyrus was the dive into Voxhollow, where he'd sprained his ankle and Bert had taken him back up to the ship.

Theo came in and shut the door. "Gentlemen, lady," he said, inclining his head at Cass with a slight smile. "I specifically invited you four in here because you know the reason we are heading back to Belhold. There is a chance we might be stopped."

Bert looked at him directly. "Like what happened near Voxhollow."

"Yes. So I want to be ready this time."

"What do you propose?"

Theo tapped the table. "Our greatest concern is Cass. By now I'm sure the House of Lords knows of her immunity and perhaps even suspects what we're trying to do. So if they try to stop us, it would be easier in the air than when we land. My question is, how do we keep Cass safe?"

All eyes came to rest on her. She fought the urge to fidget. She hated being the anomaly in the room.

"We have an escape plan," Bert said. "We have the gear, and Cass has the expertise. I doubt those who come after us will have the experience Cass has with the Mist."

"I agree." Theo moved to the desk and brought back a rolled piece of paper. He undid the ribbon and unrolled a map. Cass leaned closer. She loved maps. And this one was particularly beautiful. There was Belhold along a ragged set of lines representing the mountains. And Decadenn, pictured as a floating island. There were also places recently marked, like

Voxhollow along the western mountains. Theo's doing, perhaps?

"Bert, I need you to figure out the best way to approach Belhold. I'm hoping we can make it that far, but there is a chance the bluecoats will be on patrol. So if we are found and forcefully boarded, I'll need a place Cass can glide to and safely hide."

Bert looked at the map and tugged on his chin. "Hmmm."

"What about here?" Jeremiah pointed south of Belhold. "There's an old settlement that rarely has any Turned, and Cass could hide in one of the buildings."

Bert nodded. "That could work." He placed a finger down. "There's also another village here, a bit closer to Belhold."

"So approach Belhold by a southern route?" Theo asked, looking up.

"Yes, I think so," Bert said, straightening. "That area hardly ever has any Turned activity and plenty of places to hide."

"Good. We'll do that. I asked Cyrus to join us since he's also a diver. Depending on the situation, I want every diver we have ready. Cass will glide away first. Then, if and when it is safe to retrieve her, we will head down and rescue her."

"I'm not that good of a diver yet, but I'll do whatever I can." Cyrus's smile was almost shy.

"We'll be ready," Bert said.

Theo tapped the table. "I also want our crew to be ready. Fire drills or other preparation."

Bert nodded. "I was already planning a few of those."

"Good." Theo let out a long breath. He looked around the table. "Thank you, everyone, for your willingness to help."

Jeremiah winked at Cass. "Well, we are carrying very valuable treasure, and we need to make sure it arrives safely."

The men chuckled, but all gave her a smile.

Cass squeezed her hands together under the table. She wasn't used to so many people watching out for her welfare. An oddity. Like that puzzle box they had retrieved, housing a valuable commodity inside. She smiled back at them. Her family.

"Alright," Bert declared. "Time to get back to work. We'll have our first drill tomorrow afternoon. Cass and Cyrus, you are in charge of making sure our diving gear is in good repair. Jeremiah, I believe you have the night watch."

"Yes, Captain," Jeremiah said with a jovial salute as he stood. Cyrus joined him and together they headed for the door. Cass let out her breath and stood as Bert left the room, but Theo's hand came to rest on her shoulder before she had a chance to leave.

"Cass."

She turned. "Yes?"

"I, uh . . ." He lifted his hand and swept it up along his neck. "Could I talk to you for a moment?"

She nodded and stepped away from the door as he closed it. "What is it?"

"I want you to know I will do everything to keep you safe."

Why was he telling her this? It was obvious by everything he was doing. Including purchasing a very expensive ship. "I know."

"I want you to know I care about you. Deeply. More than I think you realize."

It took her a moment to comprehend his words, then her eyes went wide, and shock raced across her body as if she had been struck by lightning.

"I don't want you to think I only care about your blood. There's more to you than that. So much more."

He held out his hand toward her face and hesitated. When she didn't back away, he brought his fingers across her cheek. His hand was warm, and it sent more electric shocks through her body. His eyes moved across her face as if studying her, memorizing her. "If something were to happen to you . . ."

Then he tilted his face down and pressed his lips softly across hers.

After a moment, she gripped the front of his shirt and held

on, deepening the kiss. And he answered her unspoken request. He smelled like vanilla and old books. There was a fire beneath his intellectual appearance, one that ignited her own.

As they both pulled back, Cass felt her breath trying to catch up with her racing heart. She had to ask. "So what does this kiss mean?"

He gazed down at her. "I know what it means for me." He was serious now, more serious than she had ever seen him.

She swallowed. "And that is . . ."

"Cass," he fingered a curl. "I love you."

She couldn't breathe.

"I'm not one to play with a woman's heart. I've always had an affection for you, and I enjoy our camaraderie. But it has become more. Much more."

Her mind was reeling. Love. Theo loved her.

He laughed at her expression. "Is it really that hard to believe? You, Cass, are an amazing free spirit." He took her hands into his own. "And you're my friend."

The simple word hit her. Friend. She looked up into his face. Theo was her friend. The closest she'd ever had, even compared to the *Daedalus* crew. But did that feeling she had around him hold the same intensity she saw in his eyes?

"And because of that, I will do all that I can to keep you safe."

A knock at the door interrupted them. Theo opened it to Will, standing in the doorway. Cass's face warmed. How much had he heard?

"Yes, Will?"

Will glanced between them both. "I hope I'm not interrupting anything."

"No, it's fine. I was just leaving." Cass excused herself and left the cabin. She placed a hand on her cheek, her mind still reeling over Theo's words.

She could hear Theo and Will speaking as she headed

down the dark corridor. Near the door that led to the deck, she stopped. She touched her lips, remembering Theo's kiss. She thought highly of him. But did she really, truly love him? What if something happened and she was captured? Or the use of her blood didn't work out? Or the Mist took him away? So many things could go wrong. She hugged her arms against her chest. In some ways, it was harder to have people in her life than to be alone. The potential for loss was so much greater.

And yet . . .

There was also hope. A blossoming possibility of life beyond the Mist. Maybe even a life with Theo.

She straightened. That was worth fighting for, worth surviving for. And if there was one thing she had always been good at, it was surviving. The Staggs family, Luron, not even the Mist would stop her.

She'd be sure of it.

27

TWO WEEKS PASSED WITHOUT INCIDENT. THEO hadn't spoken about his declaration that day, nor did he kiss her again. But she felt his eyes every time they were in the same room or on the deck, and it made her heart go into strange palpitations.

But soon this feeling was eclipsed by something darker. Something heavy and ominous began to grow inside of her.

Cass lay on her hammock, sensing the gentle rhythmic sway as it moved with the ship, and listened to the crew sleep on the other side of the canvas flaps hung for her privacy. Someone mumbled in his sleep. Jeremiah started snoring.

She shifted to her side and stared into the darkness. She closed her eyes, willing sleep to come, but a feeling sat there inside her chest, like a lump she couldn't swallow.

She turned to her other side and curled her knees up to her chest. Nothing.

With a sigh, she sat up and swung her legs over the edge. It was almost morning; she'd just get up and start her work early. She changed into her usual loose tunic, trousers, and boots, then cinched the corset around her waist. She finger-combed her curly hair, then pulled the canvas flaps to the side.

Silently she walked between the hammocks toward the

doorway ahead, then along the corridor, up the stairs, to the main deck. The stars were still out, but the sky was beginning to change. She spotted Bert on the top deck and decided to join him.

He glanced at her as she reached the top. "Morning, Cass."

"Good morning, Bert. You're up early."

Bert shrugged. "I'm always up this early."

Cass stood beside him as the minutes ticked by, and the sky continued to change. The stars disappeared one by one, and the Mist below transformed from a dark fog to its usual greenish-grey color. Before long, the night vanished, leaving behind a sky of deep red. Beautiful, but in a portentous way. Like a great fire spread across the sky.

"It reminds me of an old sailor saying," Bert said.

"What does?"

"The sky. 'Red at night, sailors' delight. Red in the morn, sailors take warn.' It was something the sailors of long ago used to say. Back when they sailed across the waters and not the sky."

"I remember Captain Gresley mentioning something about that. I always wondered how they could do that."

"There weren't always airships in the skies," Bert told her. "Before the Mist, people would use ships similar to the *Daedalus* to travel across great expanses of water or along rivers."

Cass placed her hands along the railing. "That would be amazing." She imagined a ship like the *Daedalus* gently moving along a river like a leaf, without the gasbag. A thought struck her. "Does that mean there are other places in this world beside what we know?"

Bert nodded. "At least there used to be. Countries far beyond Belhold and Tyromourne. Even west."

"There were?"

"Yes. In fact, over the years, airships have gone in search of these other places. But no one has ever come back. So either the

Mist swallowed them up or something else happened to the airships—or they chose never to return. Personally, I think they no longer exist. We live in a very mountainous region. That's what saved us from the Mist. However, many places existed in lower elevations with no mountains. If the Mist spread, then most likely they were destroyed a long time ago. At least, that's what I think, or else we would have heard from them by now."

"Oh." Cass leaned over the railing. So much stolen by the Mist. "So what does that saying mean?" she asked, bringing the conversation back.

Bert chuckled. "A red sky at night means good weather. A red sky in the morning means bad weather."

"Do you believe that?"

"Well, I'm not a superstitious man, but it feels like a storm is coming."

Cass looked around. There were a handful of clouds. Bert could be right. She stared ahead as the sky continued to brighten, from reds to oranges and pinks. Whatever it meant, the display was very pretty.

"I'm going to start securing things just in case."

Cass turned around. "I'll help."

"Couldn't sleep?" Bert asked as they headed down the steps to the main deck.

"No. It feels like everything's been smooth so far. We have a ship, we're almost to Belhold, there could already be a cure, and we might save the world. It's too easy."

Bert laughed, then thumped his knuckles on the wooden railing. "Please don't say that. I like things easy."

Cass smiled, but she couldn't shake the odd feeling inside of her. And with Bert's explanation of the sky, it felt even more like a premonition. *Just a day or two more and we'll be in Belhold. We can do it. Nothing will happen.* She started double-checking the ropes that held the gasbag in place above the

Daedalus II. I'm just nervous. That's all.

JEREMIAH SPOTTED THE FIRST SHIP FROM HIGH UP along the ropes that afternoon. He let out a shout as he climbed down to the deck. Cass raised her head from where she had been double-checking the knots along the rain barrels. Dark clouds were starting to gather, just as Bert's red sky had predicted.

"Ship!" Jeremiah shouted. "Ship off the port bow!" He scrambled across the main deck and up the stairs of the top deck to Bert. They talked for a moment, then disappeared toward the front.

Cass dashed across the deck and also went up the stairs, intent on knowing whose ship that was. Bert stood along the railing with a telescope to his eye.

"Well?" Cass asked breathlessly.

"It's the bluecoats. I can see the flag. And there are two more ships behind them. They're still pretty far away, and the area below us is heavily wooded, not a good place for an emergency dive. Not to mention it might rain."

"So what do we do?"

Bert shrunk his telescope into a small brass cylinder and placed it back in his pocket. "We're going to make a run for it." He turned and quickly headed for the ship's wheel. "Jeremiah, alert the crew. Cass, let Theo know of this new development."

"Yes, Captain," they both replied.

Cass followed Jeremiah down the stairs, then swung right. Following the corridor she went to the captain's door at the end. She gave three brisk knocks as she felt the ship begin to turn beneath her.

The door opened, and Theo stood before her with his tunic open at the neck and his hair mussed up.

"Did I wake you up?" Cass asked, surprised to see him so disheveled.

He blinked. "What time is it?"

"Afternoon."

Theo shook his head and ran a hand through his hair. "I've been writing for hours, putting together my comprehensive understanding of the Mist into one manuscript. I started writing the moment I woke up and haven't stopped."

Cass balked. Why would he be doing that? It seemed unimportant in comparison. "The bluecoats have been spotted."

Theo jerked upright, eyes instantly clear. "The bluecoats? Where?" He grabbed his sweater off the back of the chair next to his desk. "What's Bert's course of action?"

"He's going to try to outrun them," Cass said. "Apparently the area below is heavily wooded and not good for landing. And it's about to rain, which hampers our ability to glide. Hopefully we can reach Belhold ahead of the ships."

"Rain?"

Cass raised an eyebrow. "You haven't even looked outside? A storm is rolling in. We might be able to lose the patrol in the clouds. But I won't be able to glide if it starts raining."

Theo pulled his sweater on, and passing by a hefty pile of papers on his desk, he ran a hand through his hair again and returned to the doorway. "Well, then we better outrun that ship."

Cass lifted her chin. "I believe the *Daedalus II* is up to the challenge."

They parted ways at the corridor. Theo headed to the main deck while Cass went down below to retrieve her diving gear. The reality of what was about to happen was sinking in. At all costs, this crew was determined to keep her alive. And if they were boarded, she would be forced to glide away and make it to Belhold on her own.

The very thought made her legs weaken for a moment, and she braced herself against the ship wall. *I can do this.* She closed her eyes. Soon it would be over. The world would be a different and much safer place. She just had to survive.

For Theo. For the crew. For those who live along the edge of the Mist. For—

Her thoughts steered toward the uppers in Belhold. The echelons. The undeserving.

She forced the building darkness away. "And for them, too. For Elaeros."

Cass reached the storage room and headed for the lockers, where the gliding gear, masks, and revolvers were stored. The ship shifted beneath her and lurched forward, throwing her against the wall. "Gales," she muttered as she righted herself. She could feel the *Daedalus* coursing through the air beneath her feet and see dark clouds swiftly racing by the portholes. "It really *is* a fast ship." Maybe it would be fast enough for them to reach Belhold.

Her locker was the first one. She reached inside and hauled out the glider Bert had acquired for her. Her limbs were shaking now, and twice she missed the opening for her legs.

She took in a deep breath and steadied herself. This time her motions were smooth, despite the thumping of her heart. Cass pulled the straps at the very moment the storm hit the ship.

Her fingers shook as she clasped the front of her glider. Despite her effort to focus, she could feel her heart pound along with the wind that battered against the walls. A wave of nausea slammed into her middle.

It's just gliding. You've done that before.

Cass pictured a clear day, with a bright-blue sky and fluffy clouds. She recalled the sensation of stepping off the ship and letting the air take her. The freedom as everything slipped away until all that remained was silence and flight. Just her and the sky.

She gave herself an encouraging nod. She could do this.

She checked her revolver. Six incendiary bullets in place. She holstered the weapon and grabbed a pouch with a half dozen more bullets and hooked them to her corset. Lastly, she snagged one of the water pouches. She could survive down in the Mist as long as she had a way to deal with the Turned. She was thankful there was no need for a mask. She hesitated as she glanced at the goggles, then left them on the shelf. They wouldn't be much help in a storm.

Everything secured, she started for the top deck.

28

THE *DAEDALUS* WAS A FRENZY OF ACTIVITY WHEN Cass reached the main deck. Dark clouds surrounded them, and the wind immediately sent her hair thrashing around her face.

So this was what it was like to fly into such weather. They usually avoided storms like this. But not today.

Bert yelled something, but the wind garbled his words. Then the *Daedalus* took a hard left and entered the clouds. Droplets of moisture clung to her face and skin. Cass wiped her eyes as she made her way along the outside wall toward the railing. She couldn't hear the whir of the motors or the wings over the wind.

Jeremiah ran past her, shouting something to one of the new crewmembers. She hesitated. She wasn't any good here on the deck, but she could help Will in the engine room.

She sprinted across the slick boards, slipping only once, and wrenched the door open. Will looked up from the gauges he was watching.

"Thought you could use a hand," Cass said as the door slammed shut behind her. "It seems as good a place as any to be right now."

Will nodded. "It looks like you're ready."

Cass brushed the straps along her shoulders. "Yes." Her

stomach did a little flip. "Hopefully it won't come to that." She didn't want to leave everyone behind.

"Check the gears over there." Will gestured. "They were making a creaking noise a minute ago."

The ship began to descend, causing Cass to stop and brace herself.

Will let out a low whistle. "Bert's doing a good job navigating this storm. A credit to Captain Gresley."

Cass nodded. "Yes."

The ship leveled out again, allowing Cass to move across the engine room. The noise was simply from the pipes near the gears and nothing to be concerned about.

Other than the creaking, the engines were performing beautifully, despite the strain Bert was putting them through. The *Daedalus II* really was a great ship. Her heart swelled at the thought.

Will muttered to himself as he studied the gauges. Cass continued to watch the gears move in motion, propelled by steam and oil. Outside, she could hear the wind and rain crashing against the ship. Other than the storm, it would be easy to imagine they were simply heading toward their next mission, rather than escaping a patrol ship.

A minute later, it felt as if the floor dropped, sending both Cass and Will to their knees. The enclosed gas lamps around the engine room flickered, then came back to full flame.

"Oof." Will placed a hand on the floor to brace himself. "Bert must be fluctuating the gasses in the airbag to navigate the storm."

"Definitely feels like it," Cass agreed. "I wonder if he's trying to dip below the cloud cover and soar along the Mist's edge? And how close are we to Belhold?"

"We were within a day of reaching the city. And I doubt those patrol ships stray far from their route around Belhold.

We might make it yet."

Hope blossomed inside her. They would make it. They had to.

The door opened and Theo rushed in. He shook the water out of his hair and glanced around as he shut the door behind him. "There you are," he said to Cass. "Bert's trying to get close to one of the gliding spots we talked about near Belhold."

The elation from moments ago dissipated. "So I'll be diving?"

"Maybe. We outran the first few ships, but Bert's concerned that there will be more waiting near the city. But if we can reach it . . ."

"I can dive into Belhold." It was better than diving into the Mist, which was their first plan.

"And that's why I'm here, to give you directions where to go if we can manage to get you there. Browning University is near the northern middle of Belhold, past the first two valleys."

"But we're approaching from the south."

"Yes," Theo told her. "This is just in case you have to dive into the city alone and make your way through Belhold."

"And if I end up diving outside the city?"

"Then we're back to our original plan. My first thought is hide. Hide and survive until we can retrieve you."

"What if the ship goes down?" She hated even asking that.

"If it's been a day and we haven't arrived, then make your way to Belhold and to Browning University. Ask for Professor Hawkins."

Cass's eyes slid to the floor of the engine room. Images of crossing Mist-filled hills alone, with just her revolver and her wits to keep her from the Turned, crowded her mind. Then she would have to make her way through the streets of Belhold to the university. Her heart faltered. Could she do all of that?

"I believe in you, Cass." Will's voice sounded to her right.

She glanced over and found him smiling at her.

"I do, too," Theo affirmed, his eyes holding hers. "We all do. There's no better diver or survivor than you."

Tears prickled her eyes and her heart swelled. "Thank you," she said to them both. She let out a long breath, then straightened up. "Let's go."

The *Daedalus* lurched left, sending all three stumbling across the engine room. Theo pressed his lips tight, and Will looked a bit green. Even Cass felt a twinge of nausea, and she never got airsick.

"I wonder what's going on out there," Theo said, trying to stand upright.

Suddenly, a large metal hook came bursting through the wall near the engines. Cass ducked and held her hands over her head. Splintered wood flew through the air. There were similar booms across the ship.

"What the . . ." Will gaped in disbelief. "Harpoon hooks?"

Cass glanced up. Sticking through the wall and barely missing the engines by inches was a large metal four-pronged anchor attached to a thick cord of rope. Even as they watched, the anchor pulled back through the hole, and the prongs expanded, catching the wall of the ship. The ship shuddered, and the wall creaked but held fast.

"What's going on?" Cass exclaimed.

"The bluecoats are harpooning us. It's a way to catch a runaway ship," Will said darkly.

"But I thought we outran the ships chasing us?"

"There might have been more waiting on the other side of the storm." Theo was on his way out, jaw set.

"It means they're going to board us," Will added.

Cass looked ahead to Theo, then back at Will. "So is it time for me to dive? To escape?"

"It might be," Theo said over his shoulder. "I was hoping we would get closer to Belhold. Maybe that's still Bert's idea. Let's head out and see."

Rain continued to slash across the deck, and Cass stared around her in dismay. She couldn't glide in this weather. Rain disrupted the airflow along the glider and weighed down the canvas. Even now, her glider was getting soaked.

She went back to the entrance of the engine room to watch. This storm wasn't part of the plan. What happened if they were boarded and she still couldn't get away?

There were shouts as crewmembers ran across the main deck. Cass spotted the bluecoats' ship, just off the port. It was fifty feet away and closing the distance fast.

Too fast.

Just as she grabbed the doorframe, the ship rammed alongside the *Daedalus,* throwing everyone across the deck. Fingers clinging to the framing, Cass righted herself. Her face and cheeks were cold from the rain, and her front was soaked. There was absolutely no way she could glide. Not in this weather.

She stepped back into the engine room. She would have to wait. But for how long?

From her vantage point, she was horrified to see planks appear across the railing followed by bluecoats boarding the ship. She slammed the door shut.

"What's happening?" Will called out from the other side of the room.

Cass pressed her hand against the door, heart frantically beating. "We're being boarded. And I can't make a jump in this!"

Will stood. "Then I will wait here with you until you can." He came over to her, a large wrench in his hand. Cass felt the subtle weight of her revolver at her side. But she couldn't use it. She needed to save every incendiary bullet for the Turned.

On the other side of the door, she heard the start of a battle. She glanced at the porthole on the other side of the engines.

Most of it was hidden behind the massive metal contraptions, but what little she could see was dark and plastered with raindrops.

Help us, Elaeros. Help save us all.

29

THEO WIPED THE RAIN FROM HIS FACE AS HE STOOD ready for the bluecoats to board. Other crewmembers stood beside him. "Whatever you do," he shouted over the wind, "keep them from the engine room. The moment the rain lets up, Cass will make a run for it. If you see her, clear her a path to the railing."

He turned his attention back to the planks that now spanned the space between the two ships. The first three bluecoats to cross the planks were met with fists and wooden batons. Same with the next wave. But the bluecoats kept coming until they overpowered the small line of crewmembers waiting for them.

The rain whipped around the ship, adding another layer of chaos to the fight. Theo could barely see between the rain trickling down his face and the wet hair strands falling into his eyes. He brushed them aside, then went for another bluecoat.

A crewman cried out and fell to the deck. Jeremiah was holding his own—barely—against a burly invader. One had bypassed the crew and was engaged with Bert on the top deck.

Wham!

Theo staggered as something slammed into the back of his head. He twisted around as a baton flew toward his face.

He ducked and followed up with a punch to the bluecoat's midsection. The man doubled over, clutching his middle, then fell to his knees.

Theo straightened. Then he saw a golden-masked man crossing the planks. Luron.

Theo moved to intercept him, but two bluecoats intervened. He ducked and weaved between their grasping hands and swinging batons. At an opening Theo went in with an uppercut, catching one squarely on the chin and sending him flying up and back. The bluecoat hit the deck with a loud thud and went still.

Theo took out the other with a left hook and glanced wildly around. Where was Luron?

Jeremiah had blood spurting from his nose, but his burly opponent was on the ground. One of the new crewmembers lay on the deck, groaning. The wind was still fierce, but it seemed the rain was lessening. Hopefully Cass was aware.

"Get ready," he yelled as he swiveled around, searching for Luron.

Jeremiah had thrown himself back into the melee.

A glint of gold caught Theo's eye. On the top deck. Luron was engaged in a battle with Bert.

Theo dashed for the stairs. At least Luron wasn't near the engine room. Theo only needed to help Bert. Together they would keep Luron away from Cass. As he reached the top deck, he spotted the glider on Luron's back, and his jaw clenched. No doubt the man was here to make sure Cass didn't escape, one way or another.

There was a yell, and Bert went down as Theo saw a flash of metal. Luron twisted around with his sword in his hand. Theo's breath caught. How badly was Bert injured?

Before he could react, Luron began to stalk across the deck toward him, sword steady. Theo slowly backed away, his mind scrambling for options. Debates on how to disarm someone with a sword came to mind.

First, distance.

Second, a shield.

He glanced quickly around. Nothing available.

Third, watch and wait for an opening.

Theo crouched into a fighting stance, his hands flexed and ready. He couldn't let Luron down the stairs.

Luron paused. He raised his sword. "You don't really think you can win against me," he said in that familiar voice.

Theo didn't answer. The wind, the rain, the shouts of others dimmed as he focused on the man ahead of him.

Luron slashed toward his left. Theo dodged, looking for an opening. None. He went back to an alert stance, waiting. Luron lunged forward. Theo went for Luron's arms, but the man was quick and pulled back.

Another slash, this one grazing his cheek. Theo shook off the stinging sensation.

Luron suddenly glanced over Theo's shoulder, distracted for one second.

Theo made his move. He sidestepped Luron, reaching past the sword and again for his arms. Before Luron could react, Theo had his arm immobilized. Luron tried to pull back, but Theo kept his grip. He slammed the man's hand against the railing.

Luron let out a cry, and the sword dropped. Theo kicked the weapon across the deck just as Luron rushed him.

Luron's motion caught him off guard. He fell back onto the stairs, hard.

Luron attempted to rush past him, but Theo was able to grab him by the heel. As Luron jerked away, Theo twisted around and gripped his leg. Cursing, the metal man fell forward. Theo spotted Cass on the deck. So she'd been the distraction. He just had to hold on and let Cass escape.

"Let go of me!" Luron shouted, kicking.

"Never." Theo's fingers were a vice grip around the other's boot. Cass was looking around. "Cass, run!" he hollered.

She spotted him.

"Go, now!"

"You will pay, echelon," Luron hissed and stopped struggling. His hand darted into his coat. Still gripping Luron's leg, Theo watched as if in slow motion as Luron pulled a revolver. He heard it cock. *Elaeros, help me—*

A shot rang out across the ship.

THE RAIN HAD STOPPED. CASS, ALL SENSES heightened, stood in the doorway of the engine room. It was time. The main deck of the *Daedalus* was a battlefield as the crew and bluecoats fought one another. To her right, a crewmember was struggling against a bluecoat with a large mustache. Across from her Jeremiah had his fists raised, a black eye already forming across his left eye and blood dribbling from his nose. Another crewmember and two bluecoats were wrestling on the deck. Smoke began to curl up from the tip of the ship.

Where was Theo? And Luron?

"Cass! Run!"

Theo's voice came from her left.

Cass swung her head to find Theo holding Luron by the ankle. Both men were sprawled across the stairs. Blood and water trickled down the side of Theo's face. "Go! Now!" he shouted.

Cass froze. It felt like the coward's way out to run now, especially when her friends—no, her family—were fighting for their lives. Her hand inched toward her own revolver.

Luron let out a growl and pulled something out of his coat. His revolver. Before she could scream, there was a shot, and Theo cried out.

Her heart slammed into her chest. "Theo!"

The two men toppled the rest of the way down the stairs. At the bottom, Luron scrambled to his knees. Theo was now clutching his own leg.

Cass's vision went in and out of focus. She swayed, barely hearing or seeing anything around her. Theo had been shot.

She yelled as fingers wrapped around her boot, yanking her back to reality.

Cass looked down in horror. Luron's mask had been dislodged, exposing his lower, mangled jaw. "You're not getting away."

"Yes, I will," Cass gritted out and pulled against his grip. If she didn't get away, then everything Theo and the crew were fighting for right now would be for nothing. For one moment, she almost went for her revolver. No. Those bullets were for the Turned. So she jerked her leg hard to the left, but he held on. She shot her foot back, catching him in the face. Luron yelled, and his grip lessened, but not enough for her to pull free. Their altercation had drawn the attention of the bluecoats. So close. She couldn't fail now.

"What the—" Luron swore angrily.

His grip went slack, and Cass pulled free. She ran for the railing as she yanked on the cord of her glider, releasing the canvas wings as she went.

There was another guttural cry. She glanced over her shoulder as she neared the edge of the ship. Theo held fast to Luron's boot, but his face was contorted in pain as Luron dragged him across the deck, leaving a dark, bloody trail behind.

Theo's eyes locked onto hers. "Run," he mouthed.

Cass nodded wordlessly, then turned and leapt onto the railing as her glider locked into place. Grey-green Mist spread out beneath her, with matching grey clouds above.

Elaeros, catch me!

Then she jumped.

30

CASS'S STRAPS DUG IN DEEP AS HER GLIDER CAUGHT
the air. For a moment, she stalled. Using the guiding poles, she
tilted the glider slightly downward. All of her senses reached
out around her. She could feel the crisp coolness of the air and a
slight wind change to her left. Angling that direction, a moment
later the canvas flaps caught the current, and she soared away
from the *Daedalus*.

Theo.

She took in long and heavy breaths as her mind and heart
caught up to the last few minutes on the deck. He had been shot,
and she didn't know how injured he was.

Would he . . . would he die?

She held tight to the guiding poles. Tears stung her eyes,
but she swallowed back the agony threatening to overtake her.
She had a mission, and she needed to see it through. She would
cry later.

The shouts and fighting from the ship had faded behind her.
A wisp of a cloud drew close, and Cass dipped inside. Droplets
formed along her skin and hair. When she emerged, all sound
was gone except for the rushing of air across her face. She
glanced back. The *Daedalus II* was only a speck now, hanging in

the air between sky and Mist.

Something jumped from the ship. Moments later, she could make out wings spreading out from the back as it came soaring toward her. It wasn't Bert or the other new diver. They had agreed it was best to let her escape alone. Which left only one other option.

Luron.

Panic rising, Cass gripped her guiding poles and shot forward on a new current of air. She couldn't let him catch her. She glanced ahead then down. Maybe she could lose him in the Mist.

Cass tilted her glider and began her descent toward the Mist. The greenish-grey fog rolled beneath her like smoky waves. First her feet, then her entire body was enveloped in the eerie vapor.

The Mist was thicker than she remembered it being this close to Belhold. Her heart beat faster. They hadn't flown too far off course, had they? A little further down, treetops began to emerge. A forest of old gnarled trees. Ahead, she spotted a narrow road and a dilapidated wooden bridge over a running stream.

Just then, it began to rain again.

The glider tipped dangerously forward as the water collected along it. She reached up and thumped the wings, hoping to free the canvas of the raindrops. Even more dangerous than flying in the dark, the rain would disrupt the airflow across her glider and add weight. She could stall any moment and plummet to the ground.

Sick at the thought, she only had one choice: she had to land.

Feelings of defeat threatened to overwhelm her, but she held them back. She had been through a lot worse. If nothing else, her entire life had trained her for this moment: to find a way to endure. It was time for plan B. Land and make her way to Belhold.

Glancing down, there were no open spaces except for the

road. It made for a narrow landing strip, but it would do. She thumped the glider again, then carefully angled forward. One wrong tilt and she would go crashing to the ground.

The trees were covered in faded leaves, as if the Mist had sucked all the color from them. A dove let out its mourning call. The road drew closer, along with the bridge ahead.

Her eyes went wide. Too close.

Cass pulled up on her glider, but she was coming in too fast. Wooden arches lined both sides of the bridge with metal cables and chains for the railings. She was going to hit the closest archway.

"No, no, no!" She reached for the cord and pulled. The wings began to fold in. But it wasn't enough.

Her glider collided with the arch.

Wood splintered, and the canvas tore as Cass tumbled onto the bridge. She fell to her knees and felt the awkward angle of her glider. She didn't even need to look back to know it was badly damaged.

She wanted to scream up at the sky, but instead, her fingers were working the straps before she even knew what she was doing. She struggled free of the pack and stood. Behind her were broken wings and ripped canvas. And a figure in the sky, no bigger than a fingernail, was sailing her way.

Cass picked up the broken glider and with a surge of strength, tossed it over the bridge. It hit the water below and disappeared. If she were lucky, Luron wouldn't realize she had crashed. With even more luck, the rain would take out Luron's glider. But she doubted that. The man seemed to have an excessive amount of fortune.

The rickety boards shook with her footsteps, and she jumped when she reached the end of the bridge.

She took a moment to glance around and get her bearings. Follow the road ahead or trek through the forest?

The road would eventually lead somewhere. Maybe even Belhold. There were too many chances of getting lost or running into Turned in the forest, even if it provided better cover for an escape. She didn't have time to get lost.

Road it was.

She began to run.

The road was uneven, with ruts and dislodged rocks. Weeds grew along the middle and sides, at times obscuring the path. The trees grew denser the farther she drew away from the bridge. Rain started to come down hard again, soaking through her clothes. As time went by, her breath came in short, even gasps. She couldn't imagine trying to run with a mask on.

She glanced back. No sign of Luron.

She continued on, running beneath patches of shadows so dark it was almost like running at night. At least the coverage blocked some of the rain. But what would she do if Luron showed up? Her revolver thumped against her thigh. Use her gun?

It was one thing to shoot the Turned. They were only husks with no human souls inside, driven by the spores. Shooting and possibly killing Luron involved another human being. But what if it came down to his life or hers?

Elaeros, please help me. Show me what to do.

Fifteen minutes later, her legs ached, and her soaked clothes made her shiver. She slowed down slightly and closed her eyes. The air smelled like earth and water and vegetation. Like life. With one more deep breath, she pressed on.

Not long afterward, her lungs began to burn as if she were breathing in shards of glass. Sweat and rain stung her eyes, and there was a painful stitch along her right side, which she kept a hand pressed against. Her hair hung in wet curls around her face. She stumbled over a hidden lump in the weeds and barely caught herself.

I—I can't go on.

She sucked in air between her teeth.

I have to.

Cass thought on those long days when she couldn't find food and cold nights when the flame of life inside of her wanted to go out. She drew on the tenacity that made her hold on when all seemed lost.

She would run until she fell. Then she would crawl until she blacked out.

Which considering how her vision kept blurring might not be too long from now. At least she wasn't carrying a glider on her back.

She forced herself forward. The trees were as thick as ever, with no end in sight. A lightheadedness took over seconds later, threatening to undo her. Then a fence appeared, just beyond a thick oak. Tall, iron-wrought, with the bars two inches apart. She slowed as her gaze followed the fence line to a gate.

Further down the road, past the fence and gate, dark figures appeared in the Mist. Their shambling walk gave them away. Turned.

Of course there would be Turned this close to Belhold. The Purges made sure of that.

She clung to the fence. What should she do? She looked around. No sign of Luron, and the Turned were drawing closer. She took a step back and glanced over the gate. A towering house was visible. Which meant stairs. And a place to hole up, away from the approaching Turned and Luron.

Cass rushed to the gate and wrenched it open. A loud screech sounded, and she stopped and waited, water and sweat trickling down her face, her heart racing inside her chest. Nothing rushed toward her. The rain was most likely dulling their senses.

Still, she needed to be careful.

The Mist wove between the fence and swirled around the two large columns that held the gate in place. Beyond the gate stood the two-story brick house, half covered in ivy. Overgrown bushes hid where she assumed the porch would be, and all the top windows were broken.

Not a friendly looking place. But that didn't matter. It was a place where she could hide for the time being and recover her energy. Cass stepped past the columns, then shoved the gate closed behind her. She wasn't like Theo, or Bert, or even Captain Gresley. She was short and not very strong. But she was fast. And she could think. These were her strengths. And she would find a way to use them until she could get to Belhold.

31

THE STAIRS CREAKED AS CASS WALKED UP ONTO THE porch. Spider webs hung along the ceiling, and decades of leaves and debris had collected in the corners, piled halfway up to the banister. The rain softly pattered across the ground behind her, and a sudden gust of wind moved through the trees.

Up close, the place was even creepier. This was not where she would want to confront Luron. Or—she glanced behind her at the lengthening shadows—spend the night.

She shivered. But with no idea where any Turned might be, it was safer than wandering the woods. That, and the chance of getting hopelessly lost.

She twisted the doorknob and pushed against the door. It opened slowly with a long metallic creak that echoed inside. Once there was a wide enough crack, Cass poked her head in, her hand on her revolver. There was always a chance there were Turned inside. Her eyes adjusted to the gloom, and she scanned the foyer. Nothing except for a threadbare half-eaten runner and an old clock that probably had stopped ticking a hundred years ago.

She squeezed the rest of the way inside and shut the door with another creak. If there were Turned, the sound would have alerted them. She checked the sitting room on the right. Most of the furniture was gone, along with paintings and portraits. Sometime since the Plague Wars, the house had been scavenged.

As rapidly as possible she checked the other rooms on the first floor. No Turned. Hardly anything else for that matter. That was a little reassuring. It meant that this home wasn't completely obscure and probably somewhat close to Belhold. But that also meant more Turned from the Purges. And no furniture to block the doors.

Cass shivered again and stepped back into the hallway. Time to go upstairs and check. The stairs squeaked and groaned, causing her to wince at each step. At the top, a railing overlooked the foyer below, then merged into a hallway with doors on either side. Cass checked each room, her body relaxing more and more. No Turned.

She let out a breath as she exited the last bedroom, one that had once been a child's, given the handful of painted wooden blocks and a cracked porcelain doll on the floor. She could still feel the lifeless gaze from the doll following her. There was no way she was going to stay in that room.

The rain was pelting down again, exposing the few places where the roof had holes. Cass dodged tiny waterfalls coming through the ceiling in the middle of the hallway and headed back to the stairs. Had the rain caught Luron in flight? For a brief second, she hoped so. But that would mean plummeting to his death, and she wouldn't wish that on anyone.

Cass sank down on the floor, her back against the wall, and stared ahead at the balcony. This view allowed her full observation of the front door and the stairs. There was a missing window in the second bedroom that she had marked as her escape route should Luron or Turned arrive. But there was no back gate in the enclosed area that she could see from the window. To escape, she would have to make her way around the house and back to the road.

All her options were terrible, but it's what she had to work with.

The rain ticked off the seconds as the sky grew darker. Maybe she should make a run for it, rain or no rain. Turned or no Turned.

No. Even now she could feel the dull burn of her lungs from running. And she was chilled from her wet clothes. She would wait as Theo had said to. Wait a day to give them an opportunity to retrieve her. If, somehow, they were able to glide down, this house would be a focal point. And if they didn't show up by tomorrow, she would head to Belhold alone. She was safe at the moment. And hidden.

As her heart slowed, her mind filled with images of the last couple of hours. Why had the bluecoats boarded the ship? If their mission was to kill her, they could have taken out the entire *Daedalus II* with fire or shots. It's not like they cared. They fired on the first *Daedalus* and let it burn. Was there another objective?

The front door slowly creaked open. Her heart shot into her throat, and her hand went for her revolver. Turned? Luron?

After a moment, a figure appeared. Cass didn't dare move. All she could see was the top of the head sticking past the door. It was bald, save for a handful of hair growing in patches along the scalp. The head turned right, then left. She remained motionless. She still couldn't tell if the person was a Turned or Luron.

"Here, little mouse," called out a raspy voice. "Where are you, little mouse?"

Luron.

Cass shrank against the wall. Luron was here. He had found her. She glanced at the door to the second bedroom. Should she make a run for it or—she swallowed and fingered the revolver at her side—should she take a shot?

"I'm not here to kill you." He entered and shut the door behind him. "I want to talk."

Cass grit her teeth. Right. Just talk. That's why they'd attacked the *Daedalus*.

"I know you're here. You're too smart to go running off into the woods. This is the only safe place for miles around." He began to walk down the hall. "I'm not with the bluecoats or with the House of Lords. Remember our conversation in Decadenn? I told you I would be back for your answer." She could barely hear his voice as he disappeared along the first floor.

Which world do you want to save?

If he'd asked her that when she'd been a fugitive, fleeing to avoid Purge after Purge, and if she had known then what her blood could do, she would have agreed with him. Let the Mist take over the world and start over. Or just save those who deserved it. But ever since that day in the galley when she chose to pursue what she saw in Theo and Captain Gresley, she had known she couldn't do that.

It was time to make good on her word, the word she had given to Elaeros. She would do everything she could to keep hope alive—for everyone.

Cass turned around and, on her hands and knees, slowly began to crawl to the second bedroom. She would jump down, make her way around the house, and go for the road.

She could hear Luron come back to the foyer. "So you're upstairs, little mouse?"

She ignored him as she reached the doorway.

"You can't escape. There are Turned just outside the fence. And more are arriving."

Cass paused.

Luron let out his raspy laugh. "I shut the gate, so all is safe for now. But it would be suicide to leave the manor. In the meantime, we will talk."

He had her cornered. Cass looked at the window across the room. She knew he was right. She had seen the Turned earlier with her own eyes. Her head drooped.

I don't know what to do.

The thought came to the forefront of her mind, and it scared her. Her breath came faster.

I don't know what to do. I don't know what to do. She choked back her fear. *Elaeros, what do I do?*

Rain splattered through the open window ahead. She couldn't run, and she couldn't hide. It was time to face Luron head on. She'd make her stand here and give Luron her answer. Whatever he did next would determine her steps.

Cass slowly stood. "Yes, I'm here." Her voice echoed along the hallway. She turned and approached the railing that overlooked the foyer. "And I have an answer for you."

Luron stood near the front door. He looked up, any facial expression hidden behind the golden mask.

"I don't know why I am the way I am. But I believe this gift of life I've been given is meant to be shared with others. This world and the people in it. So I'm going to do just that."

Luron placed a hand on the banister. "Even though the world has spit on you and tried to kill you?" he mocked.

Her chest tightened. "Yes."

He took a step up the staircase. "Even though they took your parents?"

Her chest tightened even more. "Yes."

"And they will never accept you, even after your blood saves their lives?"

Cass swallowed. He had found her deepest fear—that after she gave all she had, the world would carry on without so much as a thank you. Echelons would remain echelons and scavengers would remain street rats. A world that would never accept a union between her and Theo. The gap was as wide as the Mist itself.

"You're not one of them. You will never be." He reached the first landing, halfway up the staircase.

Cass brought her revolver out. "Don't come up another step."

Luron laughed. "Someone who has convictions about saving the world won't shoot me."

She knew he was right. And Captain Gresley had told her never to point a gun at something she wasn't willing to shoot. But right now there was a part of her ready and willing to shoot Luron. After all, she had to save herself.

No. She lowered her revolver. She would never shoot a human. Saving the world also meant saving people like Luron and the Staggs family, although the thought of saving the House of Lords still brought a sick taste to her mouth.

Luron reached the second floor and stood there. The sky had grown darker, leaving the house in shadows, with the constant *tap, tap* of rain. "You can join me."

Cass shook her head. "No."

"Why not? No one is here to stop you. No one *can* stop you. Both of us can simply walk into the Mist and disappear. Think of the power we have within us that we could ultimately wield over them."

"I made a promise." She lifted her head. "And my word is my bond."

Luron stilled for a moment. She could tell he was studying her from behind the mask. "You know, I was sent to capture you. The House of Lords doesn't want you dead. They want you alive. They know about your blood. And they want each of us only for their own use."

"What?"

"They are only interested in themselves. They want to ensure that only those they want to save are saved."

She looked hard at him. "Then why haven't they tried your blood?"

"They have a sample. Or at least they think they do. They generally don't keep me under observation. I took it and destroyed it. But they want to make sure your blood isn't made available for everyone. So they want you captured, to use you as a backup to me. And I can't let that happen."

There was a ringing in her ears as if all sound had been snuffed out. A fire began to burn inside her chest. Those . . . those . . . corrupt, worthless . . .

Luron's voice seeped into her thoughts. "It's really them or us. Their destruction would be a life of freedom for us . . . both."

Elaeros, more than anything I need your help right now.

Then, like a breeze when there was no breeze.

Here I am. Use me.

The words she spoke to Elaeros on the ship were a reminder of her need to help everyone. But those who would see most of humanity die had to face justice. A new way of ruling and the House of Lords abolished. Or else everything was for nothing.

Or was it?

It wasn't up to her.

"It doesn't matter." A strengthened resolve filled her. "I will only do what is right. For everybody. No matter who they are."

"Then you are no good to me." Luron's hand left the banister. "And there is no way I will allow you to be good for them."

He pulled out his revolver.

32

CASS DUCKED. LURON FIRED, AND THE RAILING NEAR her splintered. She heard the revolver click to the next chamber and dashed into the room across from her. The next shot hit the doorway, sending more wood fragments flying, followed by another shot.

She threw herself to the left and against the wall. *Think, Cass, think.* She heard his footsteps nearing. She needed to get that gun away from him.

She sidled up against the wall and braced for his entry. He would probably be leading with the gun, which meant she would need to find a way to set him off kilter—Wait. She had an idea.

Just as Luron entered, she stuck her foot out, sending him flying to the floor in a flurry of raspy swearing. Cass dove for the gun, but she was a second too slow. Luron twisted around and shot.

A piercing sting ricocheted through her right arm.

He aimed again before she could react.

Click. Click.

Relief poured over Cass. The gun was empty.

She stood, adrenaline and numb detachment shunting away the pain and shock. She dashed through the door.

Stairs or hallway?

Stairs.

Just as she turned right, something heavy slammed into her, sending her to the floor.

"Not so fast," Luron rasped above her.

Cass struggled to her knees, but Luron pressed his foot down on her back.

"I guess I'm going to have to do this the hard way."

No! It can't end like this!

With a burst of strength, Cass threw herself forward and away from his foot.

She surged to her feet.

Do the unexpected.

Instead of moving for the stairs, Cass spun around and kicked out. She caught him across his hand just as he was drawing a knife from inside his vest. He dropped it with a curse.

She kicked again, this time hitting his midsection. He doubled over as she reached for the knife with her foot and sent it sliding along the wooden floor behind her. It hit the wall, then clattered down the stairs.

But Luron was upright, lunging at her, grabbing her by the throat. "All you had to do was say yes!"

"No!" Cass choked. She reached for his mask with her good arm and began to pull. The grip around her neck only tightened, and black spots appeared before her eyes. She pulled harder until there was a metallic crack. The mask came off. Luron's hold lessened for a slight moment, and she jerked away.

She stumbled back, his mask in her hand.

His face. If possible, it looked much worse than it had in Decadenn. It was . . . hideous. Grotesque. Even worse than the visages of the Turned she had encountered. As if the corruption of his heart and mind were on display.

He breathed heavily as he stared at her with sunken eyes.

A thought struck her. He was human, just like her. An ache filled her heart. And yet there was no reasoning with him. He was bent on killing her. And if he killed her . . .

She saw Theo twisting on the ground as the Mist took over his body. Then Bert. Then Jeremiah. And Adora. If she died, they all died.

She couldn't let that happen.

One of them would be the victor today. And it couldn't be him.

The moment he moved, her body went into motion without a thought. Again, she did the unexpected and lowered her head and dashed forward. She crashed into his already vulnerable midsection, catching him off guard.

He was lighter than she imagined him to be. And like a beanpole, he could be toppled. He gripped her shoulders, but she planted her feet down with all her strength. She grappled his middle, her teeth gritting against pain throbbing along her right arm.

They wrestled there above the foyer, Cass twisting against his mass with all her might, hoping to topple him over while he grabbed a hold of her hair to yank her head back. Her vision went in and out of focus, and her scalp was on fire.

They both hit the banister, and there was a loud creak. Luron thrust her back into the wall.

Cass gasped for air but kept her hold on him. She barreled against him once more. They hit the banister again.

He jammed her head upward and back. "Time for this to end." One hand grabbed her throat and began to squeeze.

She flung her good arm up to push him away. But the pain in the other caused her to gasp.

He suddenly stilled. Down below, there was a loud thump on the door, then scraping. The Turned had made it past the gate.

One fight at a time. She wrenched herself free.

Luron came at her again, but his movements were slow and his resistance was waning.

Cass took her chance.

She gave him a final shove, sending him crashing against the banister. There was another loud crack, then the wood gave away and fell to the foyer below.

Luron's eyes went wide as he wavered on the edge. Cass tried to throw herself back, but he grabbed the front of her corset. "You're going . . . with me."

Then they both fell.

She didn't even have time to cry out before she landed on top of Luron, and their heads cracked together. Something sharp pressed into her corset down near her hip.

Cass struggled off him and lay on her back. Stars popped across her vision, and there was a strange ringing in her ears.

She stayed there, barely conscious. A faint sound of gasping breath came from nearby. Cass turned her head, but regretted it immediately as more stars flashed across her eyes. She was going to retch.

She closed her eyes and took in two slow breaths. Slowly she opened them again. Luron's form took shape, and she could see a cracked piece of wood sticking out of his lower abdomen. Blood pooled beneath him, and his face was pale, covered with a thin sheet of sweat. She looked away. The urge to retch returned tenfold. Luron had fallen on a piece of broken banister which had bypassed his glider pack and pierced his body.

There was a sharp crack, and the front door burst open. In the doorway stood two Turned. Their pale eyes roved across the foyer. Cass lay as still as possible. The only sound was Luron's rasping. But it was loud, and it wouldn't be long before they were discovered.

Slowly and quietly, she reached for her revolver. She bit her lip as her arm exploded in pain.

She carefully pulled the gun from her holster just as the Turned noticed her. She rolled, took aim, and shot.

The first one burst into flames.

Second shot.

The other Turned went down.

And now she couldn't move. Her body was screaming at her. Her head throbbed, her arm was on fire, and everywhere else ached. The Turned smoldered nearby, but the flames were already going out. There was no threat of catching the house on fire.

Cass laid back again on the wooden floor, head turned to Luron. The blood was spreading toward her, but she didn't have the strength to move away. All she could do was watch as he continued to draw in raspy breaths, each one taking a bit longer than the one preceding it.

Tears prickled her eyes, and that newly familiar heartache came back. "I'm sorry," she whispered as the last bit of life drained from his body and Luron went still. She squeezed her eyes shut, but it didn't stop the tears that seeped through. "I'm sorry," she whispered again. And meant it with all her heart.

The rain started falling again outside as the darkness took her in.

33

"CASS?"

That voice. She knew that voice, despite how muffled it was. Theo.

"Cass, can you hear me?"

She couldn't seem to make her way out of the pain and darkness. Even trying to open her mouth to respond hurt.

"There's blood. Lots of it."

Another voice. Different. She knew this one as well. Bert.

She still couldn't open her eyes, but her mouth finally worked. "Wh-where am I?"

"Cass!" A hand brushed the top of her head. "It's alright Cass, everything's going to be alright. We're here now."

"Theo?" she asked weakly and cracked open one eye. She was in a dark area with a glint of pale light coming from somewhere. "My head . . ." She winced as piercing pain erupted along her upper arm.

Theo gingerly touched her forehead. "You have a huge bump right here. And blood along your right side. But right now, I need to take a look at your arm. This might hurt a bit."

She let out a gurgled cry as Theo gently moved it.

"Sorry about that," Theo murmured. "That's a bullet wound."

"Yes," Cass mustered. Memories came rushing back: gliding

away from the *Daedalus*, fighting with Luron, falling.

She turned her head slightly so she could watch Theo. His eyes were focused on her arm, and a lock of dark hair fell across his mask. She sucked in a breath. Theo was here. And they were both alive.

He looked at her. "But I don't think it's bad."

She gave a weak smile. "That's good."

"It looks like the bullet passed through the muscle and missed the bone. There's some blood, but it's not as serious as it could be. We need to bandage it up so we can get you out of here." Theo began tearing the bottom of his shirt. Bert was examining Luron as Cyrus studied the ashes of the Turned nearby.

Her arm continued to throb. "Theo." Her mouth was dry. She swallowed. "How are you here? I thought you were shot?"

"I was only grazed." He had finished tearing the bottom of his shirt and now held up a long piece of cloth. "My leg was bandaged, and I was given something foul tasting for the pain so I could come down to get you. Sorry I don't have any with me."

"I can handle the pain." *Well, maybe.*

"I'm going to help you sit up."

Cass used her good arm to push while Theo gently helped her up the rest of the way. She held back a gasp against the searing pain.

"Now let's bandage this wound." Theo began to wrap the cloth around her arm. She winced and clenched her jaw. It hurt like gales, but she wasn't going to let him know. After he finished, he sat back. "That should hold until we get to the ship."

Cyrus crouched beside them. "I'll help you get Cass to her feet."

Together the two men lifted her slowly onto her legs with

only a small gasp escaping her lips. Cass saw Luron lying on the ground and looked away from the gruesome sight even though it was burned into her mind. "Is there anything we can do for him?" she asked.

The three men were silent for a moment, then Bert answered, "I don't think there's anything we *can* do. He's dead, and we don't have a way of moving him."

A part of her felt pity for the broken man. They had both wanted a life where Purges didn't exist and a person's merit wasn't based on their perceived worth. But he would have sacrificed the life of anyone and everyone to save himself.

"Where's your glider?" Bert asked. Theo had disappeared.

"I crashed. It broke."

He nodded in understanding.

Theo came back into the room. "She can glide with me." Cass watched as he placed a threadbare tablecloth over Luron's body. It wasn't much, but it was something.

Cass's eyes teared up. "Thank you, Theo."

He looked at her questioningly.

"For treating Luron with decency, despite what he did to me—to us."

"It's the right thing to do." He stood, staring at the covered body, his face unreadable. "After all, he was still a human being."

Bert stepped out on the porch and looked back. "Let's get going while there is still light and no rain."

Cass leaned against Theo. "Where are we heading? Back to the *Daedalus*?"

"Yes," Theo said. "Then we will figure out how to get you into Belhold."

"Why not glide there from here?"

"We might be spotted. And there would be very little protection in the air."

"But is it safe enough to head back to the *Daedalus*? I thought we were under attack."

"We were, but then that changed," Theo said. "Anyway, there will be time enough for talk later. Let's go."

With his hand beneath her elbow, Theo guided Cass outside and past the two Turned she had shot before passing out. Even the dim light seemed brilliant to her, and she blinked against the Mist. Two more smoldering bodies lay near the fence.

Leaving Luron's body wasn't any different than leaving the thousands of humans who had died in the Purges and been left to rot in the Mist. At least the covering was like a death rite of sorts.

Cass kept her grip tight on Theo as they left the old house and weed-filled yard.

Bert pointed down the road. "There's a hill about a quarter mile from here. I spotted it on our way down."

They walked between the deeper ruts, the long grass and weeds swishing against their boots. "How did you find me?" Cass asked Theo.

"It was the only place around for miles," he said. "With the rain and possible Turned around, we figured you would find somewhere safe to hole up."

They were quiet as they walked on. Cass didn't know how, but the *Daedalus II* and its crew had survived. And Theo. She thought of Luron and shuddered. Emotions warred inside her chest: warmth, relief, sorrow, and a stillness she couldn't quite put a word to.

A squirrel chattered in the trees overhead. Cass glanced up. It felt good to hear and see life in this place. Hopefully many people would be able to join the rest of life here once there was a solution to the Mist.

Ten minutes later, they reached the hill Bert had spotted.

It wasn't very long but was steep enough to hopefully give them enough speed and air to rise.

"Alright." Bert turned toward Cass. "Since you don't have your glider, we'll be tying you to Theo."

Bert pulled extra rope from his pack, and Theo smiled at Cass. "This seems familiar."

She glanced at him with a puzzled expression.

"I had to do the same thing to glide you out of Voxhollow."

"Oh." That time was still a blur for her.

Bert came up to them. "Theo, go ahead and extend your glider." Theo did as he was told, then Bert instructed Cass to step in behind. "This isn't going to be comfortable, but hopefully we shouldn't be in the air for too long. Wrap the cord around your waist, then through your legs. I'll secure you in."

After Cass finished, she placed her good arm around Theo's waist, carefully maneuvering her bad arm. The pounding in her head had receded slightly, and she took that as a good sign. Bert secured them together. "There, that should do. You're set to go."

"Are you doing alright, Cass?" Theo asked as he secured his goggles.

"Yes."

"Then ready?"

"Ready," she replied and tightened her hold.

They started their flight. Despite his long strides, Cass was able to keep up, and before she knew it, the cords around her body grew heavy as gravity tried to hold them back. But then came that moment of freedom when the air current took over.

She pressed her face to Theo's back and closed her eyes. As much as she loved gliding, it was nice to let someone else do it for a change and let herself just fly.

The flight was uneventful with little jostling, and they soon broke through the Mist. She lifted her head and spotted a handful of airships lingering in the sky a couple miles away, the *Daedalus II* among them. She wondered again what in the gales had happened. It seemed impossible that the *Daedalus* was still in the sky instead of broken pieces below.

Her head throbbed again, and she laid it against Theo's back. Those questions could wait.

THEO ESCORTED HER DOWN INTO THE HOLD OF the *Daedalus*. The area had been converted into an infirmary of sorts. Piles of blankets were laid out like makeshift beds, the wounded men on top. The lanterns that hung along the rafters were lit, and pale light streamed in from the portholes along the sides of the ship.

Both *Daedalus* crew and bluecoats were being treated. Jeremiah was working one side of the room while a bluecoat was working the other. There was an empty set of blankets next to him.

"Let's have Jeremiah take a look at your arm." Theo steered Cass through the maze of bedding. The air held a strange sickly sweet scent along with body odor and sweat. Jeremiah was slathering some kind of orange liquid across a crewmember's arm before taking a roll of linen and bandaging him up. Must be the strange smell.

Jeremiah looked up as they approached. His eyes went wide when he saw her face and arm. "Gales, Cass, what happened to you?"

"Just the usual," she deadpanned.

"Always picking fights. You really need to stop, you know," he replied with a wink. "Take a seat, and let's see the damage."

Cass bit back a scream as he lightly unwrapped the cloth.

"Sorry. I'm being as careful as I can," Jeremiah said. He examined the wound. "We'll clean this out and re-bandage it." He pulled out a small brown glass jar and a clean roll of bandages from the black bag next to him. Cass recognized it as Patterson's old bag.

"Nice bruise," he said with a grin as he began to brush the orange goop across her wound.

"Ouch! Watch it," she warned, but with a slight smile. "That's my good arm."

Jeremiah laughed. "I'd hate to see your bad one. But seriously, Cass, how'd you get that bruise on your forehead?"

"I knocked heads with Luron when we fell."

"Luron? That masked fella?" He shook his head and began rewrapping her arm. The orange serum stung but felt good at the same time. "And this?"

"A bullet."

Jeremiah let out a low whistle. "You're lucky it wasn't a bit lower and to the left."

Cass looked down. It was true. Any farther and the bullet would have gone through her heart.

Theo sat down beside her. "Cass, what happened to you down there? We still haven't heard the details."

Cass went through a shortened version of her story while Jeremiah finished bandaging her arm. As she spoke, Theo grew more and more tense. "So the Staggs family wanted you captured, but Luron didn't want them to have access to you."

"Yes. It would seem the other Families were hoping to hoard whatever immunity I could provide for themselves. And those they chose to give it to."

Theo shook his head. "And Luron decided if you weren't going to join him, then . . ."

"Yes. He was determined no one else would have use of my blood."

Theo's eyes lingered on her forehead, then he glanced at her arm as if seeing it anew. "Jeremiah's right. You're lucky the bullet hit your arm."

"Unlike your leg?" She could see the bulge just above his knee where the bandage stuck out.

Theo let out a huff. "It hurts once in a while, but it's nothing."

Jeremiah stood. "I'm going to see if there is any ice in the icebox for that swollen forehead."

"Thank you, Jeremiah." Cass watched him disappear through the doorway. "When did Jeremiah become the ship's doctor?"

"I think Patterson had taught him a few things—and was planning to teach him more."

"Oh." A heaviness descended over her heart. So much loss over the last year. "He seems to be doing a good job." She let out a sigh.

"I'm glad you're here. I was so afraid I would lose you."

Theo wrapped his fingers around her hand. His eyes were darker than she had ever seen them, and her heart went into a spasm of beats. She wanted to lean across the gap between them and give him a quick kiss.

He suddenly grinned. "Look at us. All bandaged up and whatever Jeremiah gave me for the pain is making me impulsive. And you look as beautiful as ever, even with that bruise across your forehead."

Cass laughed. "Yes, we make quite a pair."

Theo leaned back against the wall of the ship. "We made it, Cass." He continued to hold onto her hand. "We're alive, we're almost to Belhold, the Atwoods are on our side—"

"The Atwood's help is for certain?"

"Yes. Shortly after you left the ship, both Charity and her father arrived along with Captain Wyndham, head of the bluecoats. The Atwood family oversees the peacekeeping, you know, and as Charity told us, they're good friends with the captain." Theo gave her a lopsided smile, and Cass wondered what Jeremiah had given him for the pain. "A couple more ships arrived as well, all with orders to keep us safe. If not for the Atwoods, I don't know what would have happened to us. If only the other Families could see how much better it would be if we worked together."

He let out a long yawn and rested his head against the wall. "But for now, I'm just happy you're alive."

Cass gave his fingers a tight squeeze. "I feel the same way."

Theo closed his eyes, the lopsided smile still on his face. They sat there, holding hands, and eventually Cass felt his grip loosen, and he nodded off to sleep.

Jeremiah came in with a chunk of ice and cheesecloth. He glanced at Theo. "Looks like he's finally out. About time."

Cass pressed the cold compact to her forehead. Despite what Theo had said, she was sure the goose egg on her head was anything but beautiful. "What did you give him?"

"Oh, just a little something I had stashed away." Jeremiah sobered. "It was a deep graze, and it left a long furrow in his leg. The bluecoat medic took care of him. Trust me, he needed something for the pain, especially if he was going to go down and get you."

"You should have stopped him," Cass reproached.

Jeremiah only laughed. "The man was quite determined."

"I bet he was." Cass grinned and sat back. Still so much to do. Arrive in Belhold. Provide more samples of her blood. Save the world.

But for now, that could wait. She was no longer in pain, and fatigue was crashing down again. She closed her eyes and listened to Theo breathe softly beside her. She smiled to herself. She could get used to this.

34

"CASS, IT'S TIME TO GO."

Cass opened her eyes. It felt like she had only closed them for a couple minutes. Bert was crouching down in front of her. She blinked at him. "Go? Go where?"

"The Atwoods have agreed to take you the rest of the way to Belhold. And the sooner, the better. They'll slip you into the city close to the university. I'm sorry, Cass. I wish you could stay here and rest longer, but you're not out of danger yet."

He was right. Cass gently disentangled her fingers from Theo's hand and struggled to her feet. Her arm twinged at the movement, but it was bearable. And her head was no longer pounding.

Theo didn't move.

"Follow me."

Cass and Bert weaved through the bedding to the stairs and up to the deck. A plank and railing had already been placed between the two ships, and Charity waited on the other side. Night almost covered the sky, and the previous storm clouds were moving west.

She crossed the railing and stepped onto the deck of the ship. A few minutes later, the ship began to pull away from the *Daedalus* and the two bluecoat ships that hovered on either side.

Watching the ships grow smaller along the horizon brought a lump to her throat.

She just needed to be strong for a little while longer. Her fingers curled around the railing. Strong enough to finish the job.

As the ships drew out of sight, leaving only a clear, star-studded sky and partial moon, Charity joined her by the railing. Her black curls were captured in a chignon along the back of her neck, and she wore a modest traveling dress.

"How did you know to come help us?" Cass asked.

Charity stretched out her hands along the railing. "We received a post from Captain Wyndham that the House of Lords was planning on detaining a dangerous ship entering Belhold. The moment my father read the note, he hired the fastest ship to Belhold."

Cass gave her a quick glance. "Why would the bluecoat's captain send you that post?"

"Because our jurisdiction as one of the Five Families is policing the skies. The captain wanted to know why the House of Lords had put in such an order. He was already suspicious from previous orders he had received."

"Such as . . ."

"The increase in Purges, the obvious rising of the Mist with no direction for the population, plus the strange air restriction over Voxhollow a few months ago."

Cass's stomach tightened. "So your family was in charge of the Purges?"

"No," Charity said slowly. "That was the Staggs and Kingsford families." She paused. "But we did enforce it. All of our Families have blood on our hands from how we have managed the lives we were responsible for. Even a lifetime isn't enough to repay for my family's part in it."

Cass stared at the Mist below then faced Charity. "Thank

you for helping us," she said quietly.

Charity gave her a faint smile. "My family has wanted to do something about the Mist for a long time. Seeing Theo and his parents in action sparked an ember inside my father's heart, but he is a quiet and peaceful man who doesn't like conflict. He did not want to go against the others. However, when we discovered the rest of the Families were planning your capture outside Belhold, he—we—had to act."

"Did you know it was more involved than that?"

Charity looked at her, confused.

"Luron told me that the Five Families wanted the immunity of our blood for themselves and planned to administer it only to those they thought worthy."

Charity's eyes went wide and her nostrils flared. "We heard of no such thing." Anger filled her voice. "Apparently the Five Families recently have become only three. Well, it doesn't matter. It's time for a change. Between Theo's influence with the Alchemy Society and my family's oversight of the bluecoats, we'll make sure that change happens. We will have a new world."

Cass gazed into the night sky. "I hope so."

They stood side by side against the rail, each lost in her own thoughts. After a while, Charity broke the silence. "We're going to dock as close as we can to Browning University. Then I'll escort you the rest of the way."

Cass nodded.

"Cass," Charity's voice was earnest and impassioned. "We should be thanking you." Cass turned to look at her. The lights from the lanterns hung along the deck lighted Charity's face. "Thank you for doing this. If your blood truly does what Theo says it does, it will save all of us. Including my father and me. I know how much we don't deserve it."

Cass's heart went out to the young woman. She was kind and trustworthy. "You remind me a lot of Captain Gresley, the man who invited me to join the *Daedalus*," Cass said to her. "I stole from him and should have been punished, but instead he invited me to be part of his crew. I didn't deserve his kindness." She shook her head. "I don't deserve a lot of things. But his example made me want to be different. To be like him. He lived for Elaeros, so I want to as well. Wherever that leads, whatever that means."

Charity smiled back. "I can see why Theo likes you."

Cass returned her smile and then brought her gaze to the sky ahead. "And I like him." *A lot*. But first there was much to be done—if there was going to be any future.

MORNING LIGHT WAS JUST BEGINNING TO APPEAR IN the sky as Cass and Charity rode toward the university in a steamcart. The streetlamps had been put out, and those with shops or who worked in the factories were preparing for the day. The cart let out hisses of steam as it chugged along the paved street. Cass gripped the windowsill, her arm starting to hurt again. Her head felt foggy from too much adventure and not enough sleep.

But so far, so good. The Staggs family—or the other Families—didn't seem to know yet that Luron was no longer alive and Cass had made it to Belhold. Captain Wyndham was holding the bluecoats back, giving them more time to get to the university.

As they crested over a hill, the university came into view. Tall sand-colored buildings with steeples, curved windows, and manicured trees greeted them. The cart stopped before a wide gate, which was currently open, and letting in handfuls of male students, all dressed in long, dark robes and each carrying a leather valise similar to Theo's.

Cass could almost imagine Theo amongst the group, eager to learn in the classrooms ahead. Sunlight poured across a courtyard filled with vegetables and herbs, green trees, and a crisscross of pebbled walkways. Charity spoke to the guard at the gate, and he pointed to a smaller building on the other side of the square. A few of the young men glanced over at Cass with curiosity. She returned their stares with an inquisitive look of her own.

"This way," Charity said and started along one of the pebble paths. Just as they reached the middle, a young man with dark-blond hair and an entourage of other students around him approached from the left. He saw the women, and a wicked grin erupted across his face.

"Well look what we have here," he said as he approached them. "Charity Atwood. What are you doing here at Browning University?"

"William Staggs." Charity's tone barely held back its disgust.

Staggs? Cass's heart stilled as she glanced at the young man. Did he know who she was? Would he try to stop her? She was so close. Her muscles tightened.

William glanced her way and looked her over. "Who's your friend? She doesn't seem familiar. Did you find her along the dead zone?" The men around him laughed.

Cass bristled at his words and clenched her hands.

Charity touched her arm. "Cass," she urged, "go on ahead. I'll meet up with you."

At the mention of her name William frowned, but he didn't appear to recognize it. Hopefully, he didn't know she was wanted by his family.

Cass relaxed slightly. He wasn't so smart after all.

She bypassed him and his horde of young men. At the door to the smaller building, she hesitated. This was it. Inside, she would find Theo's Professor Hawkins. She would finally meet the people who had been working in secret to find a cure. Hoping to encounter someone like her.

She took in a deep breath, then proceeded inside. A long empty hallway lay before her, with a single window at the end. Tiny plaques were placed beside each door, indicating which office belonged to which professor. She read these as she passed, smiling at the thought of her own reading professors—Theo and Captain Gresley. At the third door on the right, she read, "Professor Hawkins."

She raised her hand and knocked. For some reason, this moment felt like the first time she'd stepped off the *Daedalus* into the wide-open sky. That terrifying second of free falling before her glider caught the air.

Elaeros, be with me.

The door opened, and a short man stood in the entryway. His wispy white hair stood in contrast to the black robes he wore. Thin metal-rimmed glasses perched atop the lower end of his nose, leaving his dark-brown eyes free to gaze at her. "Can I help you, miss?"

"Are you Professor Hawkins?"

His frown deepened, then his eyes went wide. He took a step back. "Are you Cass?"

"Yes."

"Oh my word, you're here. Quick, quick, come in." He held the door open and ushered her inside. "Did anyone see you?"

"Just some students. One was William Staggs." The office was a cheery place, with rows of bookcases and bright sunlight streaming through the window behind a large desk.

"Did he recognize you?" Professor Hawkins asked as he shut the door.

"No. At least I don't think so."

"He's not the brightest," Professor Hawkins remarked, evidently relieved. "Thank goodness for that. We were afraid that his father or the other Families would find you. But you're here, and you're safe. We will do what we can to keep it that way."

He unbuttoned his dark robes and hung them on a hook, then picked up a brown coat nearby. "I don't have a class until noon, so I won't be missed. And you can't stay here, not at an all-male school. So I'm going to take you to my friend's home. She lives about twenty minutes from here. In fact, she's the one that helped us figure out what your blood can do and how to replicate it." He smiled as he put on his coat. "She was never admitted into the Alchemy Society because she was a woman, and yet that turned out to be a stroke of good fortune. She would have never been able to do her research with them."

The professor's face was a mixture of emotions. "Theo and his father were right. There *was* a way to stop the Mist. Or at least enable humanity live in it." He looked at her, eyes glistening. "My dear, you have no idea how many people have been waiting for a person like you."

35

THEO'S BOOTS CLAPPED AGAINST THE MARBLE FLOOR
as he made his way to the boardroom. His body was bruised and
achy, and there was still a lengthy laceration along his leg where
the bullet had grazed him, but Dr. Turner said that overall
he was healing.

Adora, on the other hand, hadn't been able to decide whether
to be furious at him or shower him in sisterly love the night
he'd arrived at the manse. The moment he'd walked in the door,
his leg bandaged and cuts and bruises across his face, she had
embraced him with a cry, then berated him through tears. Even
Aunt Maude had been worried, in her cold, stiff Aunt Maude way.

He hadn't seen Cass since the Atwoods whisked her away
from the *Daedalus* to Belhold. Charity had sent him a cryptic
message saying Cass had been delivered to Professor Hawkins.
That was days ago, and he keenly felt Cass's absence. But he
wouldn't see her until there was a definite cure and it was safe
for her to appear again.

And the fear . . .

It hovered across Belhold like the Mist, only invisible. But he
heard it in Dr. Turner's voice, Adora's, even Hannah's. The Mist
was rising, and not even the elite could deny it now. There were

dozens of fights and riots in the city as those who lived along the lower parts of the mountains were pushing their way to the top. Life as they knew it was a sinking ship, and everyone was scrambling to remain afloat.

Which was why he had called a meeting of the House of Lords this evening, along with the key people of Belhold, who were usually not allowed to attend such occasions. As the leaders of this world, it was time for them to take charge and do what was right, something they should have done a long, long time ago. And if the other Families weren't willing, he had something in place.

Theo didn't bother to knock. He strode through the full room up to the massive table. Every chair around it was occupied, and people were standing along the walls. He recognized a few: Titus Kingsford and his sons were seated across from where he stood. Margaret Etherington was to his right, and the Atwoods to his left. Two merchants he was familiar with were in chairs, along with some members of the Alchemy Society, factory owners, Captain Wyndham, and two bluecoats. Professor Hawkins was with a woman he didn't recognize. The rest were strangers but important to the infrastructure of Belhold and with connections to the rest of the world.

Reynard nodded at Theo, and Charity gave him a quick smile. Their presence and support bolstered him as he came to stand at the front end of the table. But where was Staggs?

"What's this all about," Titus demanded, coming to his feet. "Why are these people here?"

"Because what I'm about to share affects them as well," Theo said firmly. "And they have the right to hear and decide for themselves what they will do next."

"And what about Staggs? Was he not called here?"

"Yes, he was." Theo scanned the room again. Where was Salomon—?

At that moment, the door burst open behind him. Theo wheeled around. Salomon Staggs stood in the doorway, his face dark. "What do you think you're doing, Winchester?"

"Ah, Salomon, you're just in time."

Salomon's eyes narrowed as he looked around the room. "Why in the Mist are all these people here?"

Theo ignored him. "Please, come in. Take a seat. The meeting has just begun."

"You're not the one in charge." The head of the Staggs family took a threatening step toward Theo. "How dare you call a meeting of the House of Lords!"

Theo's jaw tightened.

"He's right." Margaret Etherington rose, her monocle digging into her cheek. "By what authority did you call this meeting?"

As Titus began to get to his feet once more, Theo barked, "Sit down!"

Both Titus and Margaret sat down slowly, surprise on their faces. Theo glanced over his shoulder at Salomon. "If you are joining us, join us. Otherwise, leave. But know this, if you leave this table now"—he turned his eyes to Titus and Margaret—"any of you, you will not be invited back. I have spoken with the Alchemy Society, and they are with me. The bluecoats are with the Atwoods. And as you can see, we have members of the merchant's guild, factory owners, professors, and those in high standing with Belhold. All of our lives are at stake, and those here are ready to do what we need to, to save our world. Something the House of Lords has been remiss in doing for years."

Murmurs of agreement spread across the room. Salomon's face tightened, but he approached the table and took his seat.

Theo addressed everyone. "As you all know, the Mist is rising. Our world will be coming to an end shortly. Our family, our friends, everyone we hold dear would be Turning, except for the grace of Elaeros."

One of the merchants spoke up. "What do you mean? Do you know of a way to stop the Mist?"

"There is something even better. A cure." Theo raised his hands and gestured for silence at the sudden clamor that broke out. "What you hear next is not just for those in this room, although there are some who wanted it that way. This cure is for everyone. It will usher in a new way of living. One where people can once again spread across the land. There will be opportunities. Food and housing will no longer be an issue. Yes, there are obstacles. Current Turned will need to be eliminated. And we will need a new ruling structure. The one we have right now needs an overhaul—"

Staggs jumped to his feet. "What?" he thundered.

Theo looked directly at him, unflinching. "The House of Lords failed the people. All the people in this room are invited to help us build a better ruling authority and a better way of life. But right now, the pressing issue is the Mist." He turned to the man down the table from him. "Professor Hawkins? Please share what you and your colleagues have discovered."

Both Professor Hawkins and the lady next to him rose. A hush came over the room. "My friends, we are happy to announce we have a way to stop people from Turning. As it has been stated, we have a cure for the Mist."

THE NEXT FEW WEEKS WERE A BLUR AS BROWNING University and the Alchemy Society worked together to administer the antiserum created from Cass's blood. The first group stood near the dead zone days later, as the morning sun rose over the Mist. It was time for humanity to step off the mountain.

Theo stood near the edge, away from the others, the Mist lapping at his boots while the summer sun beat down on his head. He watched the greenish-grey fog as it rolled across the ground and into the valley. He would be the first to step inside and show the people that it was finally safe to enter. And yet years of living in fear of the Mist made his heart pound. But someone had to do it, and he wanted to lead by example.

"Are you going to stand there all day?"

Theo spun around. "Cass!"

She laughed as she stood a few feet away, dressed in a white blouse and navy-blue skirt. Her hair was parted along one side, and her curls were captured at the back of her head. The silver necklace she always wore peeked out at her neck. She was absolutely stunning. "What are you doing here?"

"I wanted to surprise you. I heard you were going to be the first one to enter the Mist." She walked up to him and held out her hand. "I thought you might like a friend with you."

He took her hand and pulled her in close to his side. "Gales, I've missed you," he said under his breath as they began to walk along the edge of the Mist.

Her eyes sparkled. "I've missed you, too. So much has happened in the last few weeks."

"Same here. You heard I met with the House of Lords and gave them an ultimatum?"

"Yes, but tell me about it."

"I was able to gather all the leaders of the city after talking with the Alchemy Society and finding they were on definitely on our side. The Atwoods did the same with the bluecoats. With the merchant's guild, factory owners, and professors there, the other Families didn't have a chance, especially since the table was opened to everyone, not just the ruling Five. It really is going to be different from now on."

"A different world," Cass murmured.

Theo tightened his hold on her hand. A different world where he and Cass could be together. That is, if she would have him.

They reached the place where a large crowd had formed, much bigger than the first group that had been selected to enter the Mist. The crowd spread across the open space between the foundations of an old factory and spilled into the streets beyond. Theo came to stand beside the handful of selected bluecoats, each one equipped with a revolver and incendiary bullets.

Even though humanity would no longer Turn, there were still Turned roaming the Mist, and they would need to be extinguished before people were finally free to live in the valleys. Cass patted at something in the folds of her skirt, and he spotted the leather belt around her waist. She had also come prepared.

Theo addressed the bluecoats. "We're all set. I'll go in first. When you feel comfortable, come join me." He noted the sweat accumulating along the foreheads of a couple of the men. One young man looked green. He knew how they felt.

Theo took in a deep breath, and with Cass's hand in his, faced the Mist. Thoughts on what it took to get to this moment filtered through his mind. The work and death of his parents. Professor Hawkins and others who labored in secret for so many years. The sacrifices of the *Daedalus* crew so he could reach Voxhollow. Cass's courage to overcome so much and let her blood be used to save everyone, even echelons like himself. Then he walked forward.

His heart started pounding as the Mist reached his neck. He shivered. Cass squeezed his hand. He took in a steady breath, willing his body to calm. If Cass could do this, then so could he.

Despite his desire to be brave, his body trembled, and he found himself holding his breath. Hand in hand, he and Cass continued deeper into the Mist and toward a grouping of old buildings.

I have to do this. I have to take a breath. I need to trust and show everyone we are safe from the Mist.

And with that, he took in a breath. Then another. And another. The air was cool and sweet. Sweat trickled down the side of his face, and his body fluctuated between hot and cold, but he was doing it. He was actually breathing in the Mist.

"I can't believe this. I'm breathing in the Mist and not Turning!"

Cass laughed as she looked over at him. "It's terrifying and exhilarating at the same time, isn't it?"

He turned toward her, grabbed her other hand, and held both to his chest. "Thank you." He closed his eyes. "Thank you," he whispered again. *Thank you Elaeros, for providing a way.*

Suddenly, Cass's lips were pressing against his. His arms went around her, and they kissed there, inside the Mist, on an abandoned street.

Cass drew away. "I love you, Theo."

He searched her eyes. "Are you sure?"

She smiled. "Oh, yes. I'm not one to play with a man's heart." Her smile grew. "I thought it was about time I let you know how I feel."

She took his hand and started leading him back toward the dead zone, where everyone was waiting. "So what do you think about sharing the captain's cabin on the *Daedalus*?"

He stopped and looked down at her. "Hold on. Are you . . . are you proposing to me?"

She glanced up at him with mischief in those bright green

eyes. "I'm just saying I've taken a liking to it. And the man who lives there."

Theo laughed, heart lighter than air. "Then I definitely propose we do something about it."

Cass grinned happily at him. "What an adventure this is going to be."

Theo couldn't have said it better himself.

EPILOGUE

THEO APPROACHED CASS FROM BEHIND AS SHE stood along the stern of the *Daedalus II* and watched the dual fans propel the ship forward. It was one of those rare days where everything was perfect. The sun was brilliant, the sky a deep blue, and the air had a cool, crisp feel to it that felt wonderful along her skin. And the fans had this mesmerizing sound that made her mind move like a pair of well-oiled cogs.

He kissed the top of her head. "Mmm, I love the way your hair smells when it's been warmed by the sun." He put his arm around her, and they stood side by side. "What are you doing?"

"Watching the fans."

"What's so fascinating about the fans?" Theo asked, bemused.

"Well, they made me start thinking." She placed her elbows on the railing. "What if we could dispel the Mist? I know we can live in it now, but wouldn't it be better to completely eradicate it? Like you originally planned?"

"Yes, it would." Theo leaned against the railing as well. "The Mist blocks so much of the sunlight, it makes it harder to grow crops. Not to mention it can be a bit gloomy down there."

"So what if we used fans or something like them to move the Mist?"

Theo regarded her with a smile. "And then what?"

"Burn it. Just like we did to the Turned."

Theo shook his head. "It's been tried before."

"When?"

"Over a hundred years ago."

Cass gestured. "Look at the technology we have now. There are fans the size of a small airship in a few of the factories and even on a handful of cargo dirigibles."

"Yes."

Cass continued, "Picture this: we use the large fans on airships and dirigibles and push the Mist into a valley, then continue to burn it. It would obviously have to be an empty valley. And some of the Mist would escape, but we could do it as many times as we needed."

Theo looked thoughtfully at the deck fan. "Yes, that might work. Since the Mist can't reproduce now that it doesn't have any human hosts, eventually the few spores left would die out."

Cass stepped away from the railing and faced him. "And since we don't Turn, we have the flexibility to keep burning the Mist until it's finally gone."

He nodded. "It might actually work. We have the tools and safety to accomplish it."

Cass grinned. "So it's a good idea?"

"It's brilliant." He kissed her forehead and started ticking away items on his fingers. "I'll need to find out where we can get fans big enough to move large sections of Mist, or have them made. And explore options for valleys. A cartographer would know best."

He continued to sort out possibilities and ideas. Cass smiled tenderly at him. Theo was still the same eager intellect she'd met a year ago, more interested in books and his studies than people. But he had a big heart. And a firm determination to do what was right and lead the new House of Lords into the future.

He was her anchor, and she was his fire. Adora said she had never heard her brother laugh so much until Cass came into his life.

She smiled at the thought. She liked reminding Theo there was more to life than books. To enjoy each day. To experience all the beautiful things Elaeros gave them.

To live. To love. To glide. To soar.

Together.

ABOUT THE AUTHOR

MORGAN L. BUSSE IS A WRITER BY DAY AND A MOTHER by night. She is the author of the Follower of the Word series, The Soul Chronicles, and The Ravenwood Saga. She is a three-time Christy Award finalist and winner of both the INSPY and the Carol Award for best in Christian speculative fiction. During her spare time, she enjoys playing games, taking long walks, and dreaming about her next novel. Visit her online at www.morganlbusse.com.

WHAT'S LURKING IN THE MIST
IS THE LEAST OF THEIR WORRIES...

THE SKYWORLD SERIES

Secrets in the Mist

Blood Secrets

Available Now!

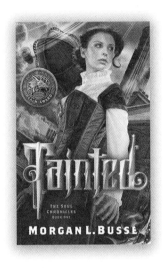 

WHAT IF, WITH ONE TOUCH, YOU COULD
SEE INSIDE THE SOUL?

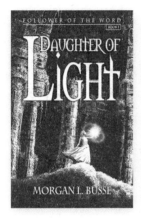  

THE FOLLOWER OF THE WORD TRILOGY

Daughter of Light

Son of Truth

Heir of Hope

Available Now!

www.enclavepublishing.com